Monkey's Birthday
&
Other Stories

By the Same Author

My Elvis Blackout

Monkey's Birthday
&
Other Stories

Simon Crump

BLOOMSBURY

First published in Great Britain 2002

Bloomsbury Publishing Plc, 38 Soho Square, London W1D 3HB

A CIP catalogue record for this book
is available from the British Library

ISBN 0 7475 5769 1

10 9 8 7 6 5 4 3 2 1

Typeset by Hewer Text Ltd, Edinburgh
Printed in Great Britain by Clays Ltd, St Ives plc

Acknowledgments

An extract from *Monkey's Birthday* appeared in *Deliberately Thirsty* Spring 1999. Thanks to Lorraine Butler, Nell Farrell, Jenny Brownrigg, Victoria Hobbs, Sean Bradley, Duncan McLean, Mike Jones and Ann & Brian for their encouragement and support.

For Steve Hodgkinson

Contents

Monkey's Birthday

Robert Salthouse lifted the glasses two by two on to the big wire rack which hung above the aluminium sink. As he raised them from their final rinse and inverted them, twin rivulets of clear warm water flowed down the underneath of his forearms and dripped off his elbows back into the sink.

First the pints, then the halves, ladies' halves, wines and spirits. The machine was on the blink again and he'd washed up and rinsed nearly eighty of the fuckers by hand. Robert fetched the blower heater from under the staffroom table. He plugged in and directed the stream of warm air underneath the rack and upwards into the dripping glasses. As they dried out and the air played across their rims, the largest glasses started to moan, the halves began to cry and the wines to whine.

'Make mine a whine,' he said out loud.

Allen came in. 'I suppose you think that's clever, don't you, Bob?'

'Yeah, I do actually Allen. Doesn't leave any smears.'

'Look, I'm sorry Robert,' Allen said mechanically, not making eye contact. 'The till in the lounge was fifteen quid down again last night. That's the third time in a fortnight and it's always when you're on. I'm going to have to ask you to go. Leave your uniform in the staffroom and I'll post you the rest of your money. Sorry.'

As a leaving present to himself Robert took the biggest bottle of Scotch he could find from the hotel's store room. Teacher's, with the label on upside down for the optics. He shoved his uniform in the staffroom bin and walked out through the lobby. Outside in the car park, he restrained himself from running his keys down the side of Allen's new Austin Princess and gobbed half-heartedly on to the windscreen instead. He went home.

Home. Partly glazed front door from pavement, mortise deadlock, Yale. Front room, inner lobby, back room, offshot kitchen, hardwood back door to knackered tarmac yard shared with next door. Upstairs bedroom one, bathroom, cylinder cupboard and occasional bedroom two. The previous occupants had done everything they possibly could to the house, except make it look nice. The estate agent had informed Robert that it was 'ripe for central heating', which meant that there wasn't any, but it did have a new roof and it was cheap. He'd paid for it outright with his redundancy money from Laycocks Engineering, his first and probably last proper job.

Ten thirty in the morning, 15 May 1982. Robert Salthouse poured himself a half-pint of Teacher's. The glass bore a frosted oval panel with the words 'Festival Ale Houses' reversed out in clear. Robert had pinched so many of the damn things from work he'd had to put up an extra shelf in the kitchen.

The first mouthful made him shudder, he felt his

stomach tighten, then the alcohol started to do its job. He relaxed, feeling the glow and accompanying sense of well-being spreading out inside him. As he poured his second half-pint Robert felt pretty good, considering that he'd just got the boot and the only reference he'd get would say 'Robert Salthouse is a fucking thief'. He'd sign on tomorrow and look for something else; it wouldn't be the first time he'd been on the sausage and he felt sure it wouldn't be the last.

Eleven. Time to go to the pub. Like many men in their mid-fifties Robert Salthouse suspected that he might be an alkie. Nowadays he just tried to keep his habit topped up, never letting it run its course but never quite mustering the effort to make it go away. He sat in pubs and got blinded so he could tell himself that it was only social drinking. He rarely kept a bottle in the house.

The pub was a real gin palace. Wards brewery had spent thousands on converting the existing Victorian pub with original fittings into a Victorian pub with 'original' fittings which they'd ripped out of another Victorian pub. They'd converted that one back into an original Victorian pub with the fittings they'd ripped out of this pub, so everybody was happy.

Wards used it as a test bed for their newest recruits; fresh-faced kids who looked no older than twelve, didn't shave, didn't drink alcohol, had never been with a woman/man, but had definitely been on *a course*.

'How are we this morning/afternoon/evening, sir, and what can I get you? Will that be hand-pulled or electric? Thank you very much sir, and here's your change.'

Robert's ideal pub was quiet, dimly lit, no women, no kids, no students, no menus on the tables, no smell of chips, no TV, no mobile phones, no pub genius, no brightly lettered blackboards bearing stupid messages, no happy hour, no quiz, no karaoke, no comedy and no carpet. A place where the landlord knew him by sight, would be pulling his pint as he walked through the door, hand him his change without a word and only attempt small talk when Robert was back at the bar for number five or six. Robert knew just such a place but it was miles away. The revamped Victorian boozer was nearest, six terraced houses down the hill and over the main road.

He walked into the public bar. Five six-seater tables and three high stools along the counter. The room could easily have seated thirty normal sociable people, but already hunched singly at the corners of four of the tables, a scattered quartet of not-normal people – with hacking coughs, well-used carriers and no regard for personal hygiene – were studiously ignoring each other.

'How are we this morning sir and what can I get you? Will that be hand-pulled or electric? Thank you very much sir and here's your change,' said a smiling youth.

Robert took his pint and sat down behind the last original Victorian cast-iron six-seater pub table in town. He lined the pint up with the ashtray, spread out a dark-green 50g pouch of Golden Virginia tobacco, a light-green packet of medium-weight Rizlas and a box of Swan matches in front of him on the mahogany surface. He rolled himself a fag.

Robert liked smoking and he liked drinking and whenever he got the chance he liked to do them both. He enjoyed the dextrous activity that was part of being a roll-up kind of guy. Cradling the Rizla in his left hand with the fold running between his fore and middle finger, he extracted a pinch of tobacco from the pouch between his right thumb and forefinger and teased it into a narrow line along the fold. He took it in both hands and tucked under the plain bottom edge. He ran his tongue along the gummed top edge and smoothed the crisp white paper into a perfect anorexic version of the genuine article. An immaculate match-thin rollie. Holding it in his right hand, Robert tapped it against what remained of his left thumbnail to make a space at the opposite end which stopped tobacco sticking to the lips. He twisted the other end up like a Chinese firework so it lit properly. He settled the rollie between his lips and struck a match.

One in the afternoon. Five pints of the hand-pulled later, the tossers from the retail park came in bragging about the size of their mortgages, putting Annie Lennox on the jukebox and ordering salad and chips with coffee. Robert sighed to himself.

Coffee? Anyone asking for coffee in a pub should be burned at the stake.

Two in the afternoon. Seven pints of the hand-pulled, the electric or whatever later, and a very drunk man put in a guest appearance. Disturbingly he was wearing a bus driver's uniform. After reducing the virgin barstaff eunuch to tears, he chose to pick on somebody way above his own size and started on a muscular young man called

Mick who was standing at the bar in Martin Dalton Roofing overalls minding his own business and trying to sneak a quick one before his next job. The room cringed in unison as the driver called Mick a poof and asked him if it was fun to stay at the YMCA. Mick only hit him once, and then only with the back of his hand, but the bus driver went down. A dribble of blood came out of his nose. The busman said how very sorry he was to Mick and maybe sometime he could get him to come and sort out his roof. Mick phoned him a taxi and decided upon a further lager.

Five in the afternoon. He didn't remember or care how many later. Robert started to hear the voices. The voices brought it to his attention that the edges of the table were filthy as they only cleaned the tops in this place. The voices suggested he scrape away that dirt. Robert set to work with a beermat which asked, 'Are you experienced?'

Five thirty. The edges of the table now forensically clean, Robert Salthouse living in underwaterworld. Shapes swimming past his table. From time to time he floated up to the surface for beer, air and cigarettes. He couldn't understand why after so much liquid he hadn't yet needed the toilet, but on the voices' recommendation he looked down at his shoes and realised that he had needed, really needed, the toilet. Several times, by the look of it.

Six. Robert started seeing things.

'What time can you play out till Bobby?' said his friend Benny, an eight-year-old who Robert hadn't seen for forty-two years.

'Long as I fucking like,' Robert Salthouse shouted out loud. 'Long as I fucking well like! Fuck you, Benny! Yer sister Margaret's a big fat tart.'

Then a woman's shrieking voice: 'If I catch you wiping your arse on my best towels again . . .'

Before Robert's eyes little Benny ballooned into the bloated and angry silhouette of his mother, cellar-door key swinging menacingly on a dirty orange string.

Her voice faded as she slammed the door. The darkness of the cellar surrounded him.

Seven. They put the lights on. Definitely into double figures. Robert stood behind a man at the bar who was wearing a jacket with the left shoulder so worn away that he could see the lining. Robert sipped his beer, taking only tiny samples now, like it was medicine. Two inches from the bottom he fell. He got a fleeting back view of the rest of the threadbare ensemble. Blue double-vented jacket, brown nylon trousers, yellow socks, white shoes.

Two minutes past seven. Robert Salthouse on the carpet. Hand over hand he made it to the door.

Outside he clawed himself upright and faced the fading light. It hurt his eyes. *Not a good sign.*

He could already taste the hangover saliva forming under his tongue. *Bad sign.*

Across the main road and six terraces up the hill, Robert found his house just where he'd left it. His vision made super-realistic by the drink, he noticed the bubbles and scars on the hastily painted front door. *Very bad sign.*

Since the day he moved in, he'd sat in his front room

looking out through furry shag-pile panes. The previous owners hadn't bothered to cut back the paint.

Bastards. Can't do anything right.

Robert went through every pocket three times; no keys. One more try for luck, and he found a pocket in his jacket he never knew existed until that moment. He panicked, thought he'd put someone else's on by mistake, then found his tobacco, papers and matches, so that was OK.

Still no fucking keys.

All he wanted was to be on the other side of that badly painted *front fucking door*.

In desperation he yanked at the brass lever handle. It came away from the door easily, far too easily in fact.

Jesus, they've even used the wrong fucking screws.

Its edges were caked with paint and there was pale bare wood underneath.

They couldn't be arsed to do that properly either, he thought, and with both hands he shoved the thing through the pane of glass closest to the Yale. Robert felt his skin puncture. Twin rivulets of warm blood flowed down the underneath of his forearms, dripped off his elbows and mingled with flakes of paint on the filthy pavement.

Tommy Hoyes sat in the musty three-berth caravan which served as his office and watched his merry band of smiling-faced, generous-spirited employees file eagerly into the building.

He'd inherited the firm from his dad. Before letting

him take charge, his father had insisted Tommy learn the business from the bottom up and work alongside each member of staff in turn. As a result Tommy had been able to meet all his future staff individually, allowing him to develop an intense and particular dislike for each and every one of them on a purely subjective and personal basis. Twenty-two of the most miserable work-shy, cantankerous, devious, backsliding, truculent, ill-tempered individuals he could ever hope to meet.

It was Tommy's extensive hands-on shop-floor experience that had nurtured the firm's unique management/workforce relationship. A symbiotic arrangement based upon mutual disrespect and non-cooperation. He needed them and they needed him. He hated them and they hated him. He didn't want to be there and neither did they. They all needed the money.

The factory was a single-storey windowless brick shed purpose-built in late 1910. Double doors at either end, a crumbling amalgamate floor and a rusted corrugated-iron roof which had leaked every time it rained since early 1911. Inside, a basic soft-drinks production line. A wheezing iron-bound CO_2 tank for the fizz. A stainless-steel dry sugar silo and green enamelled concentrate carousel for the pop.

Amy clocked in at eight, slipped into her wellies and tied on her black rubber apron. John the mechanic made sure everybody was at their posts, yanked down a corroded lever on the main three-phase box and the line started up.

Amy's job was to fish the empty bottles out of the

steriliser. It was tedious, unpleasant work. Damp, draughty and freezing in winter; suffocating, sweaty and crawling with wasps in summer.

Retrieved from cellars and pub backyards, the bottles came off the lorries crated up, stinking of stale piss. A girl fed them single file on to an articulated metal belt, the same stuff they made escalators out of but narrower and in smaller segments. It took the dirty little bottles directly to hell. The furnace. They shuffled into wire racks which held five rows eight bottles wide, passed through a sheet of boiling water, a blast of steam which fetched the labels off, then into the cold rinse. This was usually too much for the old-timers and they'd split and crumble, their shattered remains washed away down the drain and into the filter. Sometimes they exploded and burst straight out of the back of the machine; Amy's forearms were notched and scarred by years of shrapnel. When the survivors emerged shiny and dripping on her side of the steriliser, Amy lifted four in each hand, jamming them into the spaces between her fingers, and transferred them to a belt on her right which fed the filler-and-topper machine. Every fifth double handful Amy reached forward, unhooked the empty wire rack and stacked it to her left. Another belt took the filled and topped bottles past two more girls, one who slapped on new labels and checked for foreign bodies, a second who crated them up ready for the delivery lorry.

The filler-and-topper machine was unpredictable. Some days it overfilled the bottles and didn't stamp the crown tops down properly; other days it half-filled them, then smashed the tops on so hard that the bottles collapsed. Everything would shut down while John the mechanic hosed it clean, dismantled it and then struggled to repair a piece of worn-out equipment which, like everything else at Hoyes Minerals, should have been scrapped twenty years ago.

Three hours into the morning Tracey on labelling noticed a nut inside an otherwise flawless bottle of American cream soda. The next bottle was a further perfect example of pristine pop product except for the fibre washer floating in it and the one after that contained a small section of threaded bolt. She shouted for John the mechanic, who grabbed his toolbox and came running over. He got as far as a pile of empty plastic crates stacked at the end of the line ready for refilling when the woven-wire safety guard on the filler-and-topper machine pinged off. Bottles burst out in all directions, spinning and shattering on the fractured amalgamate floor. Everybody ducked down behind something large and metal. Eventually and inevitably broken glass clogged the belt which fed the filler-and-topper machine. There was a flash and a crackle at the main box as the fuse went.

Everybody was laughing as they emerged from underneath pieces of stationary equipment to the sight of a hysterical John screaming and chastising the filler-and-topper machine with a massive Stilson wrench. Without being told, they got their coats and filed out of the building.

Tommy stood framed in the doorway of the fusty

caravan. 'I want you all back here by one,' he shouted after them.

The entire workforce hit the Hammer and Pincers, big time. By twelve they'd lost the will to work and were adjusting nicely to the continental concept of the two-hour lunch break. By one they'd moved on to shorts. When they all rolled back to the factory at one thirty John had calmed down, replaced the fuse and cleared the belt, but he was still wrestling with the filler-and-topper machine. Tommy made them hang around for half an hour just to show who was boss, then sent them home.

Tommy sat in the smelly caravan and watched his employees file drunkenly out of the building.

Not a very productive day, he thought.

He'd had a couple of interesting offers from the big soft-drinks companies recently, eager to buy the business, close it down and redevelop the property as warehousing. It would mean the end of the family firm but it would provide a fair amount of ready cash and allow him to get clean away from this terrible place. The business was on the way out anyway. A good summer might boost sales in the short term but the building was decaying, the plant was worn out and none of the supermarkets would touch his stuff. The breweries were moving away from bottled softs and mixers in favour of the newer and more economical postmix system. All you needed nowadays were half a dozen pressurised carbonated water canisters, a unit which delivered a measured amount of syrup concentrate to each drink, a Wundabar keypad dispenser which controlled it, and you were in business. A rep could deliver the whole thing in the back of his car and have it set up and running within an hour. The unit fitted straight under the bar, took up zero cellar space and lasted a month between refills. Hoyes Minerals Est. 1910, No Plans for Future Expansion, couldn't compete with that. Through the half-open caravan door he could hear John the mechanic cursing the F & T machine. Tommy snapped the door to and picked up the phone.

Amy stopped at Butlers, the first café she came to, downed three strong coffees, window-shopped around town for the rest of the afternoon while the booze wore off, then caught the bus home.

She got off the red and yellow M52 Eager Beaver which dropped her right outside the house. Amy opened the front door, walked through the 12 × 12 front room, 3 × 3 lobby, 12 × 12 back room and into the 7 × 5 offshot kitchen. The house was 'ripe for central heating', so she switched on the electric fire. A relief panel of fibreglass coals, knights in armour at the front corners, two radiants above. Home. She filled the two-pint kettle and put it on the four-burner New World. Single oven, sliding pan drawer, eye-level grill. She struck a match, lit the gas and sparked up a Superking. She'd been on the bus back from town for nearly twenty minutes and she was absolutely gagging. She blew out the match and put it with the 1,603 others she'd already collected in a glass ashtray which she'd won in a raffle as part of a lager promotion.

One cup of Netto instant and three Superkings chained one from the other. Her friend Julie, who had a bay window at the front, café curtains round the back and worked as a lollipop, said Netto was scumbag city. Amy disagreed. She liked Netto. You paid your cash, you got your stuff and you returned to your dwelling.

She opened the fridge and took out a bag of mince which said 'Animal Feed Only Not For Human Consumption' in blue stencilled letters. She tore it open.

The house started to vibrate. Footsteps on the stairs like a stampede for the sales and the cat door rattling like a military tattoo. Cats emerging from under cushions, from behind the curtains, from under the chairs and behind the table. Little Fozzie from under the sink and big fat Sooty oozing out from behind the microwave.

Amy laid out fresh newspaper on the York-stone floor. As she spooned out eighteen kitty-sized portions on to eighteen kitty-sized jumble-sale saucers, she caught up with the day's local news. She only bought the paper these days because it was so absorbent and kitty teatime was the only time she ever got the chance to be absorbed by it. Local news with local angles on local stories written By local people For local people living in the local area. Things were getting ugly in the South Atlantic but in her local area the big local news was that somebody's yucca plant had flowered after twenty-five years of clinging to a miserable life in the hostile local climate.

She counted them in and she counted them out again as they troughed the mince and disappeared through the cat flap in a continuous seventeen-headed, sixty-eight-footed fluffy sausage in search of a nice soft patch of earth in some keen cottage-gardener's little paradise for a massive, toxic, plant-suffocating shit.

One short. Always the same bloody one.

Stanley, a scruffy ginger tabby. Sometimes she'd find him stranded in the cellar, sometimes trapped in the loft, often shut in the dustbin and occasionally yowling out of next door's kitchen window.

Amy didn't know, but he did it on purpose. Stanley liked to be rescued, it made him feel wanted. Show him a lead coffin about to be soldered shut until the end of time and Stanley would be straight in there, an escape artiste who didn't escape. Harry Houdini minus the punchline.

Amy checked all Stanley's favourite spots for self-inflicted confinement – no luck. Looking out the window of her 12 × 7 occasional bedroom two, she saw somebody in the knackered tarmac yard three terraces up. A man in dark-green cords and a cream cotton shirt was holding a big black pair of lacy undies to his face. He was wearing a cravat. Time to fish Frank out of the pub.

Frank. Frank oh christ Frank.

He'd swapped one institution for another, Doncatraz for the Arundel. Most of his life behind bars and the rest of it leaning against one. 'We've still got each other haven't we, Amy my love, my favourite little flump?' Frank would slur in embarrassing baby-talk after eleven pints of the hand-pulled. 'We've got eighteen lovely fluffy little flumps and we're big mummy and daddy flump and we love love love each other so much and we love our little babies, don't we?'

Well, no, Frankie, wrong on both counts actually. I'm through with you and I'm sick of all these chuffing cats. I want my little house back.

The Arundel, turn right out of the front door, five terraces down and across the main road. Amy liked the Arundel. The people from the retail park went in there sometimes and showed off but otherwise it was a nice place. Thick carpets, lovely Victorian decor and a good jukebox: Annie Lennox, Chris De Burgh, Barry Manilow, the Who. She went out through the front door and one terrace up saw Stanley licking some red stuff off the pavement.

Good, so that's eighteen after all.

Frank was propping up the bar in the Arundel as per usual. Amy joined him for a brandy and cola. He was wearing his best white shoes so he'd obviously been planning a big night out. Thankfully he'd spent all his money. Amy had only to mutter the magic words 'sausage, egg and chips' to get him outside and they were soon heading back home, Frank wittering about a fight and some geezer who'd pissed himself and fallen down right behind him.

Home and a Lateshopper carrier on the doorstep. A bloodied Stanley inside. He was still warm but he was dead. Frank was crying like a baby. A Biroed note on the back of a Martin Dalton Roofing invoice.

'Sorry i kilt yor cat it was an accidunt my pone number is hear sorry.'

Amy put Frank to bed. She kissed him and stroked his face until he nodded off. Then she tied up the carrier and put Stanley in the bin. *Seventeen to go*, she thought.

'Get out of that one, you silly little sod,' she said out loud, then doubled up, crushed by unexpected and overwhelming grief.

Red robot digits said 11.30. The radio came on. Nella hit the snooze for the eighth and, she promised herself, the final time. Late for work again. 'Shit, just ten more minutes,' she moaned, and rolled over on her brand-new posture-sprung mattress, underpinned by an eleven-month-old Victorian cast-iron bedstead almost paid for from the Freemans catalogue decked out with ivory satin sheets and pillowcases by Deesyr of Tinsley and topped off with a 100 per cent cotton Mariella handcrafted heirloom throwover with intricate embroidered battenburg lace detail from Great Universal's autumn collection.

Eleven forty. The radio came on again. Somebody's yucca plant had flowered after twenty-five years and radio local were creaming their jeans about it.

Swinging her legs off the bed, Nella slipped into a red silk dressing gown by Deesyr of Tinsley, wriggled her toes into fluffy pink slippers and wiggled across five feet of patterned 20/80 acrylic-wool-mix carpet into the bathroom. She undid her robe and let it fall away, exposing her naked form to the admiring gaze of the massed collection of ceramic dolphins which inhabited every available surface. Then she shed the slippers and stepped into the shower. As the first jet of water hit her back she started to wake up and smoothed her tandoori-tanned face and neck with gel, also by Deesyr of Tinsley. She moved down her shoulders and went to work on her enormous breasts.

She gelled the uncharted and unseen area underneath and worked, worked, worked her fingers down along her broad hips and into her inner thighs. Unlatching the showerhead from its chrome bracket on the powder-blue tiled wall, she opened herself with one hand and cranked up the control on the power shower to eleven on the Richter scale with the other. Nella applied its gushing head to her vagina and in exactly forty seconds was doing a very passable impression of Slim Whitman's 'She Taught Me How to Yodel'. Oh, the wonder of modern plumbing technology!

She then worked on her huge distended gut, the mystery area below that, and used up all the rest of the gel on her massive and monstrously sagging arse. Twenty-five years old and twenty-five stone. Nella was fat. Very, very fat. It wasn't glandular, it wasn't psychological and it wasn't anything to do with her upbringing, it was because she ate way, way too much. Comfort eating, she told herself, too close for comfort eating. All the time.

Nella stepped out of the shower. Forty-two little pairs of dolphin eyes watched in awe as she towelled herself dry and slipped into the long black 50/50 wool-polyester-mix dress she'd got out of the Grattan catalogue. No time for make-up today, she was already very late. Down the stairs and into the 12 × 12 front room. Plaster aristocast

Louis Quatorze fireplace, coal-effect gas fire, pretend marble hearth, polystyrene ceiling rose, plastic chandelier, a suite which looked like it was made out of the offcuts from a padded cell, striped burgundy paper below a plaster dado, framed dolphins on the daffodil-yellow walls above and a white typewritten envelope on the mat.

Dear Ms Crasnovsky,
It has recently come to my attention that your cheque account is currently £350 overdrawn against an agreed Credit Zone facility of £200. Kindly do not issue any more cheques until your account is back within the agreed credit limit. Please pay in the balance within the next five working days. Your account has been debited with an additional administration charge of £27 for the preparation and processing of this letter.
Yours sincerely,
R. Prior
Manager Natwest Bank Meersbrook branch

Nella's surname wasn't really Crasnovsky. Crasnovsky was a Polish name. Nella came from Grimsby. She had a father, a mother, a brother and a sister who also came from Grimsby, all with the surname of Davis. Nella's surname was also Davis. However, a distant member of the family was indeed from Poland. His surname really was Crasnovsky and he had a terrible secret. He'd come to this country in the fifties and set himself up in business shot-blasting and repainting the fair city's fleet of trawlers with a revolutionary new paint process. It turned out that it was a revolutionary new water-based paint process. The little boats looked lovely in dry dock but, three days out on the icy seas towards Murmansk, the salt water would eat up their thin freshly scoured hulls with a vengeance. They went down in large numbers. Nobody ever thought to blame it on the paint.

Nella liked the idea of being a feisty hot-tempered Polish babe, she thought it would make her more interesting, so she adopted the surname of Grimsby's most notorious innocent and unconvicted boat sinker, and now her imaginary moniker was on the wrong side of a completely unimaginary financial fuck-up.

Nella went back upstairs. Dispensed with the black number and strapped on a plunge bra.

That should do the trick, she thought and selected a further outfit. Leopardskin. Not off a leopard but a lecherous little ferret on the Wednesday market. No knickers. Tight skirt. Tiny top.

Twenty minutes later she squeezed herself through the gap between Allen's shiny new Austin Princess and the staffroom wall. It looked like Robert had beaten her to it today, but she gobbed on the windscreen anyway to give his snotty spittle a little female company and walked into the lounge.

'You're an hour and a half late,' Allen said, not looking up from the bandit.

'Oh, I'm soooo sooorry, Allen! It's my time. It feels like my womb's falling out through my fanny today.'

She only had to mention her privates and Allen would

go to pieces. He hit the wrong button on the bandit, which for once was the right button. Fifteen quid.

Looking up from the bandit, Allen focused on Nella and took in the outfit.

'Erm, would you come into my office for a moment, love? To discuss, erm, your overtime.'

One day while looking for a new till-roll in Allen's office, Nella had found a magazine folded into one of the ledgers in his desk drawer. There was a picture of Mount Fuji on the cover. She thought it might be a holiday brochure. Red letters said, 'Mountain Climbing for Beginners DP Special.' Allen on a climbing holiday? In Japan?

Well, I never.

The only way Allen was going up a mountain was in a forklift chairlift. On page one a photograph of a lady, five men and a walnut dining table. It looked like a shot from the Argos catalogue apart from the fact that the lady was very fat and wore no make-up; obviously not a professional model. Naked and spreadeagled on the dining table, she had a penis in each hand, one in her mouth, one in her vagina and a further penis inserted into her rectum. Her face, breasts and bloated stomach smeared with stale jism. The soles of her feet filthy. The men still had their shoes and socks on and looked clinically bored.

Nella wasn't shocked or even upset by this discovery, in fact it made her laugh. She knew what she looked like and she also knew by now that if a strange little man about a quarter of her weight started to take an interest, it wasn't only because of her magnetic personality. Some blokes were just made that way. She knew just how to deal with Allen now. It explained a lot of things. Why she'd got the job in the first place, faced with such stiff dolly-bird competition, and why Allen sometimes looked at her like he'd had his brains sucked out the back of his head by the lager pump. *The larger lady. Double penetration. Well, well, well.*

Allen sat down on the greasy blue-grey nylon-covered swivel chair he'd got from Office World. Nella knelt and unzipped his brown 30/70 nylon-wool-mix trousers. She extracted Allen's penis from his jockeys, 100 per cent cotton. They had a picture of a strawberry on the crotch and a motto which said 'BITE MY CHERRY'. There'd been a mix up at the pant printers and Allen had got twenty pairs for four quid from Dinnington Sunday market.

Nella felt his cock harden in her mouth and Allen started to whimper. She ran her tongue around the edge of his helmet for a few moments and he began to gasp obscenities at her. Mainly about her being fat, her being a fat slag and her being a fat slag who was begging for it. Nella tickled his testicles with the fingernails of her left hand and Allen went into overdrive. Now he, big fat, barely human Allen, was the world's greatest lover. She carried on like this for about a minute while he told her what kind of a sexy guy he was and then she started to bite him halfway down the shaft of his dick. He was really shouting now. She hoped that Robert could hear. Robert despised Allen and she knew that he knew what was going on. A wave of Allen's stinking sour-milk bollock odour washed over her and she felt sickness rising from her stomach. From bitter experience Nella knew exactly what to do next. She eased her right hand under Allen's plump and sweaty buttocks, inserting the first inch of her thumb into his rectum. It was like pressing the fast-forward button on a video and not a very good video either. Almost immediately Allen came into Nella's mouth. About 15 ml of it. She spat the stuff out into a battered copper-coloured waste bin screen-printed with a hunting scene, a leftover prize from a raffle which had been part of a lager promotion and was situated two feet to the right of Allen's mahogany-effect desk. Allen zipped himself back up.

'Aw thanks Nella, that was lovely. I'll put an extra fifteen in your wages this Friday.'

First time she ever did it he gave her twenty. The next time she'd filled her mouth up with ketchup from the Family Dining Experience restaurant. Looking down, Allen had felt half his cock in Nella's mouth and seen a red rivulet running along the remaining portion, dripping off his bollocks on to the carpet. He'd run screaming around the office and fallen over the waste bin. Allen only ever gave her fifteen after that.

'Oh, by the way, Robert's left us . . .'

'OK see you later Allen.'

She changed into her uniform. Two seventy-five an hour and fifteen quid for two minutes. A salty taste in

Nella's mouth. Couple dozen more of those and the overdraft would be well under control.

Poor Robert.

Five thirty in the morning. Earnest Griffin snapped awake, the hysterical screams of regimental sergeant-major 'Mad Jack' Harris ringing in his ears. Saturated with sweat and guts churning it dawned on him that there were all kinds of things he should have done in preparation for today, the big day, and had not.

Buggering Aida, what a fucking relief.

He remembered he wasn't in the army any more. He started every day like this, a few seconds of half-conscious, sphincter-splitting, brick-shitting dread followed by a wave of sudden and fully conscious relief. Elation. Joy. No guard duty today. No square-bashing today, no latrine detail today, no spit and polish today, no getting shot at by the krauts, the wogs or the micks today, no chinless wonders telling him what to do all day and no regimental red-tape bullshit today or any other day.

Earnest stepped into threadbare Y-fronts and for now, left it at that. There was work to be done.

He stripped his bed, unhooked the curtains and put the whole lot into the bath for a soak. He unscrewed the light bulb, breathed on it and gave it a thorough polish with his favourite duster, a fluffy orange number with a black line drawing of Chatsworth overprinted with 'Historic Derbyshire' in stiff red ink. He raised the bulb up to the curtainless window to check for smears and saw his face reflected back in its shiny curves.

He ran his duster around the upper edges of the picture rail, the moulded architrave and the skirtings of the 12 × 12 front bedroom just to make sure that no dust, dirt or cobwebs had dared to appear anywhere since this precise moment in time yesterday. Then he washed it, rinsed it, wrung it in the bathroom basin and spread it on the radiator to dry. Earnest's house wasn't 'ripe for central heating', he had a Myson pressurised combi-boiler in the kitchen, a Honeywell motorised three-way valve in the cylinder cupboard which no longer required a cylinder, and a Stelrad Supreme bolted to the wall of every room in the house. Copper 22 mm feed, 15 mm return and a thermostat in the front room permanently set to wonderfully warm, completely cosy, superlatively snug. Oh, the wonder of modern plumbing technology.

No more freezing barrack-room dormitories for him, ever. He opened the door to the cupboard formerly known as the cylinder cupboard.

'What the –?'

A scruffy ginger tabby came belting out of its purple interior, shot past him and legged it down the stairs.

Fucking cat!

Earnest flicked a switch and the pump kicked in with a satisfying mechanical whirr that sounded like the engine room of a modern supertrawler. He got his spare toothbrush from the bathroom cabinet. Earnest started work on the floor. In earnest.

Two hours later and the lino shining like new, Earnest stood by the bed stiff to attention while the brass inspected his handiwork.

Seven thirty, and through the thin bedroom wall he could hear her from next door moaning in her sleep.

Nella. Those tits, that arse, that tight leopardskin outfit, those tits, that arse. Bloody Norah.

Earnest's Y-fronts bulging like Y-not-Fronts. Regulation British Army wank. Bathroom. Basin. Pants around ankles, cock grasped firmly in right fist. One two one two one two. Explosion of sperm into the plughole. Time for a tea break.

Stand easy chaps, you may smoke.

Earnest marched himself downstairs to the kitchen, filled up the big aluminium kettle from the cold tap and stuck it on the cooker. He went into the 12 × 12 front room and sat bolt upright on the green two-seater, rapidly diminishing penis weeping into his worn-out shreddies. Regimental photograph framed over the tiled fireplace. New World radiation gas fire, highly polished chrome surround. White walls, shiny bare bulb, green cottage suite, scrubbed bare boards. Monster high-fidelity stereo sound reproduction system, Linn Sondek LP12 deck with moving magnet Ortofon VMS 20 Mk2 cartridge, twin Radford valve amps, a passive Audio Innovations pre-amp with a Cambridge Audio balanced power supply, bi-wired with QED braided sixteen-strand low-loss oxidised copper cable to Ruark Talisman speakers, Slate audio stands, gold-plated interconnects throughout. Shelves either side of the chimney breast housing fifteen albums colour-coded, cross-referenced and in alphabetical order. The complete recorded works of Slim Whitman. No further decor. He stared at the window, which would be requiring a proper clean later.

Earnest could teach that chap two doors down a thing or two about the correct procedure –

– *windows, for the cleaning of.*

His windows were in a deplorable state, filthy and covered with paint. *Disgusting.*

Twenty minutes and not even a trace of a whistle later, Earnest returned to the kitchen, turned on the ring and lit the gas. This time the kettle boiled and he made fifteen mugs of very strong tea, one for each member of his platoon. He saluted his reflection in the kitchen window, drank his tea in one and began to cry.

Earnest poured the other fourteen away down the enamel sink. He wouldn't mention that last bit to his counsellor. All things considered, after thirty years in the forces he'd adjusted to civilian life pretty well.

Earnest washed the tea things and lined up the mugs on the drainer. As he raised number fifteen up to the light to check for smears, warm water flowed down his forearm and dripped back into the sink.

Upstairs. A shit, a shave and a shoe-shine. Earnest dressed carefully. Shiny brown brogues, soft moss-green argyle socks. Dark-green corduroy slacks, stiff brown belt. He selected a freshly pressed long-sleeved 100 per cent cotton cream shirt, fastened all except the top two opaline plastic buttons and latched the cuffs with his regimental souvenir cufflinks.

Earnest paused and slid open his sock drawer for a

second time. *Why not?* he thought, *got to keep my spirits up somehow.*

He reached past two rows of socks neatly rolled into pairs. Behind them a frilly lavender-filled bag his sister had sent and beside that a black .38 Webley service revolver. Earnest gently extracted his most prized possession. Rust-coloured silk shot through with cerise and so soft you'd hardly know you had it on. A cravat. It was just like the one Mad Jack wore when he hit the casual wear at weekends. Exactly like it. It was it. He'd had to bribe that orderly a tidy sum to get it for him but looking at it now, glowing in the weak sunlight, it had been worth every last penny.

As Earnest smoothed the silk around his throat, he felt his penis trying to break out of the shreddies again.

Blimey, down, boy.

That was a bit worrying. He held Jack in high esteem, everybody did.

That was as far as it went, honestly.

Better not mention that to his counsellor either.

Time for his fags and the paper. Earnest checked his reflection in the full-length mirror which hung in the 3 × 3 lobby at the foot of the stairs. *Crikey, who is that handsome bastard?*

He marched up the hill.

Zero eight hundred hours precisely. Earnest arrived outside GT News Gleadless Road branch. He dodged into the doorway of Pat's Quality Fruit & Vegetables as the paki came out to set up the newspaper hoarding. The paki stood it at right angles to the pavement, unclipped the metal grill and carefully smoothed today's headline on to the backboard. Then he snapped the grill shut and went back inside.

Black felt-tipped capitals. 'Local Yucca Flowers After 25 Years, full story and photos.'

Earnest tiptoed into the shop. The paki had his back to the counter refilling the fag shelves from brown cardboard cartons.

Perfect.

'Earnest Griffin, Corporal Queen's Own Rifles Catering Corps, serial number three eight six one three four, reporting for duty sarh!' he bellowed.

Rajesh suffered minor heart failure, turned to Earnest and flashed him a cheesy grin. Earnest thought he looked pale this morning, pale as a paki could ever look anyway.

He reckoned that Rajesh was a decent enough chap. He had been playing this game with him every single day for fifteen months and Rajesh always gave him a smile. He was a hard worker, kept the shop spotless and always opened dead on eight. Earnest liked him for all of the above.

Those Indian chappies made damn fine soldiers.

Rajesh turned his back again, reached down twenty Senior Service and scooped a roll of extra strong mints from the sweet rack. He cut the string from the bundle of papers with a stanley knife, the two halves of its grey metal handle lashed together with brown parcel tape, and handed Earnest the top copy. Rajesh smiled and Earnest smiled back. Earnest left the exact money on top of the till, spun stiffly on his heel and marched out of the shop. They'd only ever speak the day after a budget.

Blimey, O'Reilly, the price of fags on the outside, nearly three times what they charged in the NAAFI.

Back in the street, Earnest pocketed the fags, prised open paper-covered foil, popped in an ESM and jammed the rolled-up newspaper into his left armpit. He marched off down the hill.

Halfway down, Earnest encountered a crumpled magazine lying on the pavement. A picture of Mount Fuji on the cover. He thought it might be a holiday brochure. Red letters said, 'Mountain Climbing for Beginners DP Special.' Earnest Griffin on a climbing holiday? In Japan?

Well, I never! That would be fantastic.

He turned back the cover with the toe of his gleaming brogue. The lady was obviously not a professional model.

Home, Earnest unlocked the front door. He was gagging but refused to smoke in public. He tore the cellophane off the Senior Service, sparked one up with his Do or Die souvenir regimental Zippo and spread out his paper on the kitchen table. He read every single word.

Local news For local people written By local people in Earnest's local area. They'd given over five pages to grainy black-and-white photos of the yucca and an in-depth article about its initial purchase, formative years, miserable blotched teenagehood and final glorious fruition into mid-twenties flowerdom, penned by the local gardening correspondent who gardened locally somewhere or other around here. Each time he stubbed his fag out in the glass ashtray, which he'd won in a raffle as part of a lager promotion, Earnest popped in an ESM, stood up and went to the bin. He picked the butt out between his thumb and forefinger and dropped it in.

Goodbye, old friend.

Then he rinsed out the ashtray, dried it with the teacloth and held it up to the light to check for smears.

First time he opened the bin a scruffy ginger tabby exploded out of the confined space and Earnest shooed it through the back door. Then he returned to the table and sparked up a further Senior Service. Fifteen fags, fifteen ESMs, fifteen trips to the bin, fifteen rinses, fifteen dries and fifteen smear inspections later, he'd completed the crossword.

The answer to each clue was contained within the day's top story and today fifteen of the answers to the ten acrosses and the ten downs was a single word. The Y-word.

The monster stirring in his trousers again.

Nella.

Quick march up the stairs. The bathroom. The basin. Slightly more imaginative freestyle British Army Overseas Wank this time. Right hand her mouth, forefinger her tongue playing around the edge of his helmet, him gasping obscenities and a thumbnail starting to bite him about halfway down the shaft of his dick. His hand getting tired now and he feeling a bit ashamed of himself, Earnest knew from bitter, lonely and desperately frustrated experience exactly what to do next.

He eased his left hand under his sweating buttocks and inserted the first inch of his thumb into his rectum. It was like pressing the fast-forward button on a video and from where Earnest was standing a pretty good one. The stuff squirted into the plughole. A narrow jet from a kid's waterpistol. About 15 ml and much waterier than last time. He cleaned himself up with the bog roll and dropped sticky crumpled tissue into a battered copper-coloured waste bin screen-printed with a hunting scene. He'd won it in a raffle, part of a lager promotion.

Eleven thirty in the morning. Time for Earnest's constitutional. He was exactly the kind of man who would have suited a dog. He could have called it Jack. He would have loved the dog and the dog him. It would have welded itself to his heel and lived to be a very happy, very old dog. Its dying thought would've been *I love Ernie.*

If Earnest had gone first, his dying thought would've been *I love Jack.*

But unfortunately it was not to be. The mess, the noise, the hairs, the dribbling and the inevitable little accidents. It was unthinkable.

Twice round the park, then just a quick one.

Cutting through the hotel car park, Earnest stopped to admire a shiny new Austin Princess.

Jesus H, some dirty bastard's gossed on the windscreen and more than once by the look of it.

Noon. He marched into the lounge and there she stood in all her glory. Behind the bar, his goddess. The object of all his lustful sweaty big-tit-oriented, shaking-fat-arse-enhanced oral wank-based fantasies. *Those tits. That uniform. That arse. Lummey. No other customers. Perfect.*

'Good afternoon, Allen, I'll have a cold glass of gravy with a hair in it please.' He smiled. She smiled back.

'What . . .?'

Earnest raised one eyebrow and flashed her the best smile in the whole history of the civilised smiling world.

'You've got the boss's badge on love.'

They had a laugh about that and the fact that Allen was at an important meeting wearing a girl's name badge. Earnest got himself a lager and purchased a cola for the lady. He settled in at the bar and told her a few stories about his army days. Looking her straight in the face, he could tell from her eyes that she didn't believe a word of it, which was just as well really as they were made-up stories anyway.

Something about her face today . . . A fleck of shiny stuff on her cheek caught the light and looked for all the world like a dried-up bit of spunk.

No. Surely not.

Nella ate every single peanut out of the nibble dishes ranged along the counter. Earnest desperately trying to maintain eye contact – his gaze dragged continually downward by the irresistibly powerful forcefield of Nella's magnificent cleavage.

Nella thought Earnest was hanging his head. She liked that. She thought he was bashful, a real gent. And such a snappy dresser. *Those shiny brown shoes, that tight little bum. That permanent throbbing bulge in those sexy green cords. That silky cravat. Oh my word!*

Nella refilled the nibble dishes, immediately gobbling their entire contents, her own special presence refreshing parts of Earnest that a further lager and another cola for the lady could never ever have even begun to reach.

One in the afternoon. Earnest loved her and left her. He went home. Things to do, curtains to clean, windows to wash.

He filled a bucket from the hot tap, added a dash of vinegar to the clear warm water and took a cloth from the line. He did his front window, thought, *What the hell*, moved one terrace up the street and did Nella's as well.

Two in the afternoon. Job done. Earnest carried the bucket back along the entry and tipped its cooling contents down the drain in the knackered tarmac yard which he shared with next door. He pegged the cloth on the line, inverted the empty bucket and sat.

The open air. He sparked up a further Senior Service. Nella's line looked like Mardi Gras. Gaily coloured tea-cloths, pastel bath towels, stripy leggings, flowery T-shirts and then the metal line prop, a rusted nine o'clock watershed, followed immediately by an in-depth, strictly adults-only, black underwear drama-documentary containing language which may offend. Crikey. Earnest unpegged a huge, wide-screen spectacular pair of knickers by Deesyr of Tinsley and pressed them to his face. A thong at the back and an open-weave lace panel round the front.

Just a thong at twilight. Wowee.

His cock standing to stiff attention and his mind running amok. *Get a grip, soldier, this really does have to stop. Ask the woman out.*

Three in the afternoon. Earnest picked up the bucket and a scruffy ginger tabby sprang out from underneath it, yowling at him as it flashed past.

He fetched yesterday's paper from the kitchen. Back

along the entry and round the front. He scrunched up the first double sheet, an article about an Austin 1500 starting up first time after being garaged for the past twenty-five years, and used it to polish his front window. Polished it up until you couldn't tell if there was glass in it any more. He moved one terrace up.

Four in the afternoon. Nella coming up the road wearing the wild-animal outfit and Earnest rubbing away at her window more vigorously than strictly necessary, something else on his mind.

'Aw thanks Ernie. That's very nice of you. Why the newspaper, though?'

'The newsprint lubricates the glass love. Little trick I picked up during the service of Queen and Country.'

He smiled and she smiled back.

'Windows – correct procedure for the cleaning of. Earnest Griffin, Corporal Queen's Own Rifles Catering Corps, serial number three eight six one three four, reporting for duty and at your service marhm,' he bellowed.

Nella suffered minor heart failure, then flashed him a cheesy grin. She looked pale this afternoon, pale as she could ever look under that tandoori tan anyway.

'I suppose you think that's clever, don't you, Ernie?'

Ascending left eyebrow. Award-winning smile.

'Yeah I do actually Allen. Doesn't leave any smears.'

Red robot digits said 7.30. Ken rolled over in his bed and the radio came on. A local yucca had flowered for the first time in twenty-five years. *The stupid cunts are having a field day.*

He reached over and got his fags off the melamine bedside unit. Ken flipped the cardboard top back with his thumb and extracted an Embassy with his front teeth. He sparked it up with his see-thru green plastic lighter and inhaled deeply. Instantly he was seized with an overpowering and uncontrollable urge to take a dump.

A sharp pain jutted across his midriff and he threw back the Blades quilt cover. Ken shuffled body-hunched and buttock-clenched across five feet of 20/80 polyester-wool-mix carpet into the toilet.

He lifted the lid, eased down his pyjama bottoms and sat. Bent double with his chest pressed against his knees, he felt his guts drop what seemed like at least fifteen feet and the faeces started to gush out of his anus. Solid stools at first, then another sharp pain. A cocktail of watery mucus and bubbly brown froth exploded all over the white porcelain rim and splashed up on to the underside of the antique pine-effect lid.

I'll have to sort that out later or Mum'll go nut-nut.

Galloping trots followed by some thinner stuff, less like diarrhoea and more like chronic underwear-destroying wind augmented with occasional lumps. Ken blew chunks for several excruciating minutes and then the fountain dried up. He unfurled a yard of white Netto Supersoft and started to clean himself up. Two yards later, he baby-walked to the basin, trousers around his ankles. He wetted a wad of tissue under the hot tap and used it to clean any stray bits of stuff attached to the matted dark hairs around his rectum.

Ken held the last piece up to the light. He checked for smears.

Whiter than white.

He dropped it into a copper-coloured waste bin screen-printed with a hunting scene. His mum had won it in a raffle. Part of a lager promotion.

Pain gripped again and he sat. A further quart of warm brown fluid squirted out of his ring and Ken was forced to repeat the whole procedure.

Somewhere inside Ken's bowels a gauge, a round black dial with a red needle, jammed hard up against a stop underscored by white letters which said 'Empty'.

Downstairs, a carrier containing a smaller bag formerly known as the Sunblest Bag. Inside cobs, an apple, a Mr Kipling and a cola.

Mr Fucking Kipling. He really does make exceedingly small cakes. Cheers, Mum.

Outside. The bus appeared and Ken climbed aboard.

Ken picked up his carrier containing cobs cake cola and stepped off the red and yellow M52 Eager Beaver. He crossed the road and went up two flights of concrete steps, dipped through a revolving door and entered the big grey Community-Service building.

Dead on eight. Ken signed at reception. Went out through the back door and sat in the painting van. Ken settled himself on a slatted bench which ran the length of the Transit and tried to make himself disappear. He felt an overwhelming sense of relief. If you had any sense and there was still a space, you really needed to get in a painting van. Gardening vans were OK so long as it kept fine. 'Fence Posting in Mexborough, Murder Capital of South Yorkshire' vans were really not so good, they made you clear the ground first with a strimmer. 12cc of raw two-strokin' petrol-driven wire-whippin' ear-splittin' grass-cuttin' power. First pile of dog shit you skimmed the crust off atomised, blasted directly into your face, your nostrils and, worst of all, your mouth. That could really take the shine off a Mr Kipling.

Three pairs of hands holding three different tabloids: *Sun*, *Star*, *Sport*. Silence. Ken heard posh cackling laughter in the car park, then felt the Transit shudder as the two smart-arses climbed aboard.

'Oh, shit,' he said under his breath.

They looked genuinely pleased to be there. A skinny bloke with a big fat nose, spots, and a daft grin permanently glued to his ugly face. A very tall girl, beaky, with short black hair. She was wearing green Pepsi Cola overalls which she never tired of telling everybody her stepdad had got for her, and Docs. She had a faint Brummie accent. They always brought a radio with them and never forgot their sarnies. They'd spend the day smiling at each other, talking in funny voices, laughing and pulling faces. They were obviously in lurve. They spread out a copy of the *Guardian* across their four knees and started babbling excitedly about its contents. Ken sneaked a look. It was a black-and-white photo of the skinny big-nose spotty bloke starkers and lying under a pile of wet leaves. The girl had taken it, she was supposed to be an artist and the picture was supposed to be an art work.

Boss man Harry opened the front door, sighed and slid into the driver's seat. He greeted the smart-arses warmly like they were life-long employees and totally ignored everybody else. They could hardly wait to show him the photo and he murmured several appreciative phrases. The girl said something using a word Ken had never heard before and the big-nose spotty bloke made a witty remark using two more. The three of them started to laugh. They went on like this all the way to the community centre, chattering away like old friends.

Got there, parked up and they all filed in. Harry unlocked the mess-room door and put the kettle on. The two smart-arses made tea for everybody and then Harry said what was doing today.

'Right,' he said to the smart-arses. 'You two are on glossing today because you're so good at it; you other two are on the walls. Ken and Glyn, you're on the tower because you're such fucking idiots. We need to get that ceiling coated up. Quickly as we can.'

Glyn had a tattoo on his forehead. Grey-green letters which said 'snikS'. Round his throat a dotted line and more blotchy grey-green letters which said 'ereH tuC'.

He'd executed his own art work in the reflection of a shiny stainless-steel Doncatraz toilet, right after he'd sold his trainers to big Shaun from C-Wing. Fifty pee up, rest of the trip wearing hand-crafted cardboard and gaffer tape flopflips. Long dyed blonde hair in a scruffy ponytail and a red Dodgers baseball cap deliberately backwards on his head.

A head full of more lying bullshit than any sane person could possibly handle.

Harry set everybody up with gloss, emulsion and brushes, then hung around while Ken pieced together the tower, impeded and annoyed by Glynn, who seemed to think he was site foreman. Every time Ken snapped a section of scaffolding into place, Glyn patted it lovingly with his hand and gave him the thumbs-up.

'Cooking with gas now Kenny, job's a good'un.'

Eventually, and accidentally on purpose, Ken cracked him a nice one with the end of a pole while Harry wasn't looking. Glyn rubbed his arm and clapped his hand on to Ken's shoulder.

'See that line there, Kenny?'

'Er, yeah.'

'Well, last week I were fishin' canal basin and a pike bit mi arm off. I had to get a taxi up to 'ospital and on way there it bruk down so I 'ad to take engine out and fix it up. They sewed my arm back on but you can't see stitches coz they're all on the inside.'

Ken could never bring himself to challenge any of Glyn's bullshit, he figured it would be like kicking a cripple. The skinny smart-arse bloke had no such qualms.

Harry had put him on glossing with Glyn one time and when the skinny bloke produced a tin of baccy to make a roll-up and offered him one, Glyn told him what a waste of money it was as he grew his own tobacco, pressed his own papers and manufactured his own tins.

'Righto,' said the smart-arse. 'I'll have half a pound of

tobacco, some of your fine papers and five Glyn-type tins this time next week. Do you accept cash?'

Glyn made an excuse and slunk away muttering that he was a jumped-up little cunt. Ken agreed. It was true. He was.

Ken knew from painful experience that it didn't do to bullshit those kind of people. He got no pleasure from it. They'd look at him with a mixture of pity and contempt, making a mental note of everything he said for a great big posh laugh behind his back later on. He became increasingly aware that his accent sounded like wet bread and the useless stories would die on his lips.

Ken finally got the tower set up, trundled it into place and locked up the wheels. He finished his section of the ceiling in ten minutes and he sat, dangled his legs over the edge, sparked up an Embassy and relaxed.

Glynn was trying to obliterate a stain on his bit of the ceiling and after three coats and no luck he was muttering about a special new-formula emulsion which he'd invented last week.

'It'd cover a poxy stain like this in one. No fucking problem.'

A further Embassy and Ken couldn't take any more. He climbed down from the scaffolding and walked to the end of the corridor. He flicked on the lights. The shadow vanished.

'Hey, I think I've cracked it,' Glyn shouted. 'Cooking with gas now, Kenny! Job's a good'un.'

Lunchtime and Glyn trying to ponce fifty pee off anybody with a pulse to get some chips. Silence from all the real people and then a financial contribution from the smart-arses.

Ken ate the sarnies, drank the cola and saved Mr Kipling for later. Meantime he watched as the smart-arses laid out their stuff. Sandwiches, salad, crisps, french bread, pâté, dips.

'Cunts,' he mouthed at Glyn.

They really weren't dealing with this in the approved manner. They had a further big posh laugh with Harry, made tea for everybody again and had an in-depth conversation about the colour scheme and the gratuitous use of gravy brown.

Harry actually took notice, got on the phone and started shouting about the gratuitous use of gravy brown, put the phone down and went back over to the smart-arse bloke,

'Sorry, but we have to use that colour, so now it's a straight choice between that and prison.'

'OK,' said the smart-arse. 'I refuse to apply that particular hue Harold, for artistic reasons you wouldn't possibly understand. Cuff me and take me down.'

Harry laughed. 'All right, use the green instead, but if I get any shit from the clients I'll refer them to you.'

'OK,' said the smart-arse. 'If they prefer that brown, I'm referring them to a psychiatrist. It's colours like that that make people do crime in the first place.'

Afternoon. The smart-arses had the only radio in town and they absolutely refused to put the football on. Every single week Ken promised himself he'd fetch a radio and every single week he forgot.

Kenneth was a present dweller. He'd think of something. It would be the best and most satisfying thought he'd ever experienced. Ten minutes later it was gone.

First time he ever did a burglary he got all the stuff on the pavement outside, then realised he had no transport. That time he was lucky: he'd picked up a bunch of keys in the house and one of them fitted and started the nearest car.

Ken nicked an acoustic guitar once. It had nylon strings and wasn't nearly loud enough. So he fetched the green plastic-covered wire his mum used to tie up her clematis from the cellar and strung the guitar up with that. Much louder. Then he watched as a fissure flickered across the neck.

Next day Ken opened the case and the guitar had imploded. Turned in on itself like a crisp packet under the grill. He'd gone one up on that fucker Pete Townshend. Ken had devised a guitar that smashed itself up.

Ken got bored with the disappointment each fresh break-in would bring. Nobody had much worth nicking, maybe a decent TV and video, sometimes a midi-system and a bit of jewellery. Occasionally they'd surprise him with some medals or a coin collection, but mostly it was strictly small-time.

He'd started getting into people's houses just to see what was going off. He broke into the old bag's house one door down, it was like a museum and cold as the fucking grave. Ken shortened the chains on the kitchen sink and bathroom basin by one link and, experiencing a rare thought about the future, laughed himself senseless imagining the consequences.

Last time Ken did a burglary, he didn't even get out of the house. One night in the pub he overheard a group of students bragging about how little money they'd got left after blowing their grant cheques on stereos and TVs. Ken thought student houses might be a good bet. If they'd all got stereos and tellies and you found a house where five of them were sharing, there'd likely be five of each – some of the richer ones might even have computers. He followed them home to a terrace much bigger than his mum's, nearer town and opposite the football ground.

Next day, mid-afternoon, Ken knocked, just to make sure. If anybody answered he'd be sorry but he'd got the wrong house. Nothing. A battered blue Transit parked outside, but no sign of life. Ken wriggled through the cellar grate, the tried and trusted method of the slimmer junior housebreaker, crossed the damp cellar and climbed a flight of slab stone steps. He entered a back room through the cellarhead door.

The place was unbelievable: plates of half-eaten food, pizza boxes, cans, mugs filled with green fungus and dog-ends, clouded milk bottles sprouting light-brown fur. Mottled back damp halfway up the walls, and everywhere the stink of fetid socks. He poked his head into the kitchen and breathed fresh air.

The back door was wide open.

Ken tried the front room. It was even worse: more half-eaten food, a ruptured beanbag, a rotting vinyl suite, a carpet that looked and smelt like reconstituted vomit and a tangle of severed wires where a TV and video should have been. Two bulging bin bags in the centre of the room. Ken never saw who hit him, but when he came to – four hours later – the bags were gone and he was surrounded by a furious gaggle of second-year engineering students all demanding to know where he'd hidden their stuff. It was almost a relief when the police came.

The afternoon dribbled away punctuated by a smart-arse-administered teabreak, a Mr Kipling and a further Embassy.

Five. They all got back in the Transit and dragged back to the sinister grey building. For reasons known only to himself Ken introduced a half-empty tub of Leyland Brilliant White Vinyl Matt Emulsion into his carrier.

An M52 appeared and Ken got on. He sailed past his mum's house and up the hill.

Time to get some lovely, lovely chippies.

A big knackered sign said 'One Thousand Spartans Fish Restaurant'. Leaning up against the flaking T, a grotesque black-and-white figure in leather body-armour bearing a lozenge shield and a trident. A smiling cartoon haddock was impaled on the end. An upside-down badly painted Union flag. Traditional English Fish end Chip. Freshly Mad Pizzas. Run by 100 per cent Liverpool Chinese for the 100 per cent good people of South Yorkshire.

Ken got himself a cone of chips and an ironic fishcake – bright-orange batter, nought per cent fish. He wandered back down the hill.

Level with the military man's billet, Ken was all done. He stuffed the greasy paper through the letter box.

That should get the fucker going.

His mean desert eyes singled out the bright lights and earthly delights of the Arundel bar, grill, taverna and discotheque.

Through the double swing door. Ken hoisted his saddle over broad manly shoulders. The piano player paused mid-ragtime, a sea of faces swung around and four bad motherfuckers at the bar flicked back their overcoats to reveal twin pearl-handled Colts. Doc cheap package Holiday. Jesse interest-free credit one week only James. Staggeringly reduced – buy now, pay next September – Lee and Billy – crazy prices everything must go – the Kid.

Who was that handsome stranger?

Dead-Eye Kenny – bad Community-Service hombre, Colt .45 and a deck of cards – loosened his black leather holster a couple of notches and ordered himself a pint of best sipping electric.

Three pints later and Ken was thoroughly bored. Time for a kip. He headed off back to the ranch. Outside the old bag's house he paused, levered the top off the emulsion with his key and plunged his right hand into the paint. Ken left a blotched white handprint in the middle of her front door.

He didn't know why.

Seven thirty. Adeline sat bolt upright in her big wooden bed and switched on the wireless. A Bakelite Philco People's Set c. 1935. Two minutes later it warmed up.

There was a really interesting programme on. All

ITCH
6759 6314XX XX6651
EXPIRY DATE 09/02

****	TOT	6.49
EPS		6.49
CHANGE		0.00

nsaction in accordance with
ted terms and conditions

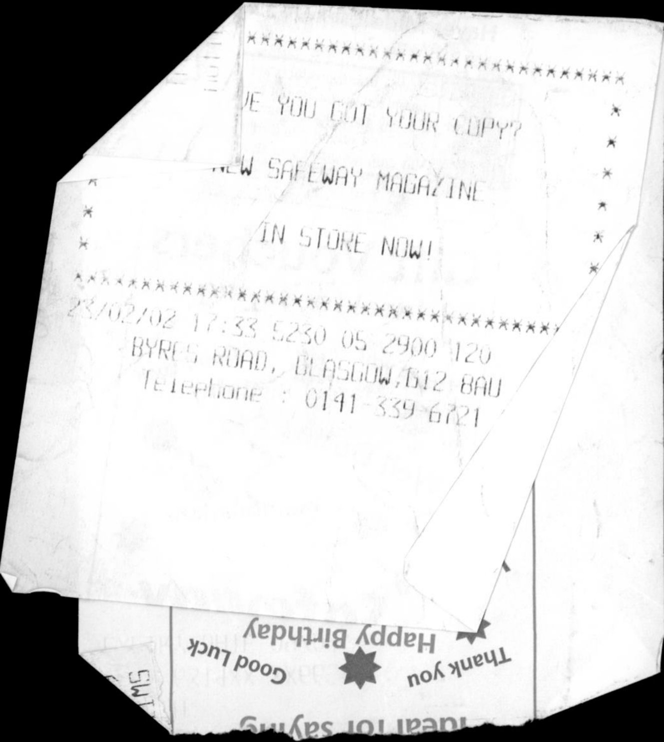

...E YOU GOT YOUR COPY?
...EW SAFEWAY MAGAZINE
IN STORE NOW!
23/02/02 17:33 5230 05 2900 120
BYRES ROAD, GLASGOW,G12 8AU
Telephone : 0141-339-6721
Ideal for saying
Thank you
Good Luck
Happy Birthday

about growing tropical plants in a hostile climate. She flipped open her marbled notebook bought from the post office, and took notes. c. 1920 Swan Morton fountain pen, eighteen-carat nib, bronze ebonite body. Beautiful copperplate handwriting, 15 May 1982.

Adeline slipped into her brand-new slippers from Sunwin House, popped on her silk dressing gown and smoothed back the crochet counterpane Catriona had made for her in the early seventies.

She drew back the voile curtains and saw a shiny line of driverless Austin Princesses sliding backwards level with the upstairs sash window of her 12 × 12 front bedroom. Cream walls, chocolate woodwork, polished floorboards the colour of demerara sugar and a coffee-coloured rag rug. Adeline went downstairs and entered the 12 × 12 front parlour. She pulled back the drapes, heard the sharp hiss of air-assisted brakes and saw another row of backward-facing brand-new Princesses slide past the front window. The transporter trundled away down the hill on to the main road and turned sharp right by the Arundel.

The kitchen. Adeline opened up the damper on the range, an embossed copper sunrise and raised cast-iron letters which said 'Century Cooker 1900'. She used a battered T-bar to lift out the cast-iron bung and a blast of hot dry air washed past her face. Adeline shivered and rattled glowing anthracite back to life with the poker. She filled the four-pint Empire-ware kettle from the brass bib tap over the Belfast.

Adeline set the kettle on the hob. Twenty minutes later

it burst into song. She hotted the pot, spooned in three good ones, filled it with boiling water and left it to brew for five minutes.

Eight o'clock. Best drink of the day. Adeline poured herself a nice cup of Lifeboat.

One for Terry too. Her mester and best-ever pal. Dead for nearly twenty years now, but she always poured him a cup.

There'd been an accident at Tyzack's the day of his retirement. He'd fallen into the unfenced galvanising bath. His workmates watched helplessly as the eyes and teeth exploded out of his head and his screaming face dissolved for ever into a vat of seething electrolyte.

She'd been to the presentation afterwards to get the clock and Tyzack's had paid for his funeral. The box was pretty much empty.

But it was a lovely send-off.

Adeline thought about him every single minute of every single day. When she dreamed it was of her and Terry. Nineteen, laughing and running down a hill in the sunshine, legs going so fast they couldn't stop. Mostly she woke up smiling.

Adeline picked the paper from the mat and sat at the scrubbed spruce table in her cosy kitchen. There was a fascinating gardening article.

Adeline went back upstairs. Late-nineteenth-century Crossley runner, brass stair-rods, nickel clips, scumbling on the treads and risers. She fetched her marbled notebook and bronze fountain pen. She made further copperplate notes.

Adeline washed up china tea things in the Belfast stoppered with a white rubber plug which had a worn, and newly repaired, chromium-plated chain.

After almost ninety years of continuous use the old one had shrunk overnight. That nice young man Ken from next door, who occasionally did odd jobs for her, fitted her a new link so it reached the plughole again.

Adeline dried china with a white linen teacloth – blue stripe reversed out with white letters which said 'glass cloth' – and stacked them in the little ivory-painted pine cupboard next to the range. Over the Belfast a calendar for 1963. A bleached-out picture of Whitby harbour with each day crossed out until Friday 15 September, the day time stood still for Terry.

Eight thirty. Adeline went back into the front parlour. Marblised slate fire surround and mantel, brass crucifix to the left, Tunbridge-ware trinket box to the right. Terry's clock in pride of place.

Tiled cast-iron insert, battered brass fender. Monstrous Bush radiogram. Red distempered walls, tall cream skirtings, thin green picture rail, bronze picture hooks, ancient faded, foxed photos suspended on chains. On the chimney breast a fine sentimental watercolour of a little girl with flowers in her hair playing in a rose garden with a tiny tabby kitten.

Indian rug, bergère suite, crocheted cushions by Catriona, black japanned china cabinet loaded to the gills with unused Carlton-ware, a wedding present more than half a lifetime ago. Original box-sash, brass closure with spherical white ceramic knob. Thick velvet curtains, mottled bamboo rail, brass rings, hollow copper finials.

Adeline made up the fire and switched on the radiogram. She and Terry-in-the-head settled down to some serious knitting for 'Our Boys in the South Atlantic'.

Peace. Comfort. Solitude.

Two thirty. She fetched a box of Mr Kipling Fondant Fancies from the kitchen. Time to go see Catriona.

Two doors up Adeline knocks. No answer. A thud from inside the house. Tries the handle and the front door swings open.

'Cat, where are you, Cat?'

Adeline sees her old friend's face poking out of the 3 × 3 lobby at floor level. Smiling.

'Blimey, Cat, what you doing down there? We only cleaned that carpet yesterday?'

Red blotched legs sticking out at an unnatural angle, dark bruising to her face and purple welts on the inside of her left forearm. Strong smell of Cat-pee.

Adeline goes over, touches Cat's forehead.

Good. Still warm, still breathing.

'Catriona, are you all right?'

Catriona's eyes flick open, she scrambles into a sitting position and drags herself upright with the handrail.

'Crikey Addy, I must have blacked out again. I don't think anything's broken. Put the kettle on love, and I'll join you in a mo.'

Percy woke up, got out of bed when he felt like it and didn't turn on the radio. He went downstairs and screamed at Catriona until she made him a cup of tea. After that he shouted some more and she went up the hill to get his paper.

When she came back, he threatened her until another cup appeared. Percy spat on the floor and spread out the racing page on the scrubbed pine table in the 9 × 7 kitchen.

He stirred in four sugars and pressed the spoon against the inside of Catriona's forearm. Hot EPNS seared soft flesh, she squeaked with pain and Percy laughed. He had no idea why she still got caught out, he'd been doing it every day for the last forty years. Just his little joke. He loved his wife, but mostly he acted like he hated her. Really hated her.

Percy studied the form and made his selection. He shouted at Catriona. She seemed unwilling, so he twisted her arm up behind her back until the tears came. She made another trip up the hill. To Ladbookies.

On her return Percy had to slap Catriona quite hard to get some breakfast, and when she finally came to join him at the table with her cuppa, Percy whipped away the chair from under her. Catriona sat heavily, far too heavily, on the cold lino floor. Shock waves rolling up her spine, hot tea scalding her legs and she screaming fit to bust. Percy thought it was hilarious. Married life was such a laugh.

Upstairs. Percy shaved, dispensed with maroon dressing gown and tartan slippers. He applied the blue serge two-piece, cream 100 per cent cotton shirt and light-brown sixteen-pearl-button Dunn & Co. waistcoat. He laced on black Church patent shoes.

Stick. Ash with a grey rubber stop, a collapsible umbrella bungied to it in case of inclement weather. Percy didn't need a stick. Eighty years young, all his own teeth, a head of wiry white hair, fit as a violin and twice as handsome, it came in handy for emphasising points of conversation.

Downstairs Catriona washed up breakfast things, then came up to make the bed.

As she entered the bedroom, Percy shouted, 'Catch!' and his stick caught her full in the face.

'Butter-fingers,' sang Percy.

He picked up the stick, got his slippers and left the room.

Pausing to tuck his slippers under the second step, Percy went downstairs and strode out the front door. Partly glazed, two solid panels, brass letter plate, Yale, mortise deadlock, chrome numbers which said '19', black Dolphin knocker.

Catriona sat on the edge of the bed and wept. Her face wet and sore. She lay down for a snooze.

The Arundel.

'Pint of electric. Today, if that's all the same to you, sonny,' Percy brandishing the stick and barking at the twelve-year-old to put the telly on.

Two hours three pints later Percy checks his watch. Two twenty-nine.

Any minute now . . .

Two thirty. A knock at the door. Catriona woke up.

Adeline.

She smoothed herself down and set off down the stairs. Something under the second step.

She fell.

Four thirty. Earnest marched up the hill. A further pack of Senior Service, an additional roll of ESMs and the evening paper. Rajesh's wife behind the counter this time; her red bindi reminded Earnest of Jack Harris. A mark like that at the front and a crater the size of a nightclub ashtray around the back. Earnest found him in the toilets. Twitching in a puddle of his own blood. Gun still in hand.

Back in the street, Earnest pocketed the fags, prised open paper-covered foil, popped in an ESM and jammed the rolled-up newspaper into his left armpit. He marched off down the hill.

Halfway down Earnest encountered a crumpled magazine lying on the pavement. A smiling blonde on the cover eyeing a huge courgette. He thought it might be a cookery magazine. Red letters said, 'EASY, CHEAP AND VERY TASTY.'

Well, I never! Earnest Griffin cooking up a super meal? For Nella? Fantastic.

He turned back the cover with the toe of his gleaming brogue. The lady was obviously a very good cook. Making sure nobody was watching, Earnest scooped up the magazine, rolled it inside his paper, jammed the paper back into his left armpit and went home.

Home, Earnest unlocked the front door, went through

the front room to the kitchen, unrolled the paper, extracted the magazine and smoothed it flat on the table. He tore the cellophane off the Senior Service and sparked one up in Jack's memory. He began to cry.

Get a grip, soldier! Tonight may well be the night.

Earnest dried his eyes on a crisp Irish linen teacloth and sat at the table. He read the magazine from cover to cover. After mature consideration the final plans for Operation Nella were drawn up. Earnest decided upon:

Starter: Wilted Spinach Mandarin.
Main Course: Antipasto with Marinated Mushrooms.
Sweet: Praline Pumpkin Tart.

Piece of cake. Easy, cheap and very tasty.

Next thing was to get the ingredients. First off, Earnest decided to secure, to ensure, to certify, the main, the very special, the most important ingredient. The lovely lady.

One terrace up he knocked. She opened and their eyes met. A pink nylon baby-doll slashed to the waist, absolutely no other garments.

Oh, sweet Jesus!

Dry-mouthed, limp with desire and struggling to control a stammer which hadn't afflicted him since his schooldays, Earnest said his piece.

'Earnest Griffin, Corporal Queen's Own Rifles Caca Catering Corps, serial number three eight six one three four, reporting for duty and at your suh-suh-service, marm,' he croaked.

She flashed him a cheesy grin.

'Would madam care join me in a sussussimple yet nourishing repast to be served at 20.30 hours precisely? That's half past eight this evening to you, love.'

'Aw, thanks Ernie, that would be lovely. See you half eight.'

Earnest marched off down the hill, his mind reeling with ingredients, recipes, unusual serving suggestions, fresh ideas for pretty place settings, possible repartee and impossible sexual positions.

Bottom of the hill, turn left at the main road, two hundred yards and Netto. Outside, a woman got up as a giant lollipop wearing a 'Julie' name badge and handing out free samples. Inside, music piped 'Una Paloma Blanca'. Earnest's mind went completely blanca and he began to perspire. They didn't have any of the stuff. Salt, sugar, flour maybe, but apart from that . . .

Not one single flipping item.

Earnest found himself marooned at the end of an aisle which featured matching 400 g tins of animal food: SuperCAT and SuperDOG. The pets' heads badly excised and superimposed on yellow stars, making them look like Jewish pools-winners.

Earnest perched on a pallet precariously piled with polythene-packed pedigree poodle pellets. He pondered. He panicked. He speedily scotched a Survival Supercurry solution. He'd surmounted similar situations on several successive Saturdays. It was the same scenario, you had to utilise unusual and unfriendly limited local conditions. Learn to love the lie and lack of the land.

Left right, left right, left right. Crikey, hold it right there, soldier, this is serious. What's left? They do tinned stuff, they do frozen stuff, right? And there's still time to hike up yonder hill, peruse and possibly purchase Pat's Quality Fruit & Vegetables produce. Yippee.

Just then Earnest had a visitation, an intense gut-wrenching moment of complete clarity. He heard a rasping semi-hysterical voice. Jack. RSM Harris. Nutty as a person who made hats for a living.

'Do yer special Ernie, go on, do her yer special.'

Looking up, Earnest saw a minature Mad Jack hovering above the washing-powder aisle, sporting a disposable nappy, a mottled green fatigue jacket and his gorgeous cravat. Something wrong with this picture. Earnest took a deep breath and swallowed hard.

Behind the Huggies mobile an enormous photo of a bunch of asparagus neatly secured with a rust-coloured elastic band. Better not mention that to his counsellor.

Earnest bought two 340 g tins of Meteor 100 per cent corned beef, produce of Brasilia. One 326 g tin of Farmers Fayre sweetcorn in water, sugar and salt added, packed under licence by Nabisco Ontario. One 411 g can of Courtina Fruit Cocktail, produce of various countries, contents may settle in transit, specially packed for Netto and one 500 g family-sized tub of Ye Olde Devon Churn Raspberry Ripple, manufactured by Jacksons of Dewsbury, heavily fortified and enhanced with every E-number so far discovered by mankind. Earnest paid his cash.

Outside. Julie the giant lady lollipop lunging around the car park pursued by a crazed mob of small children, an overexcited Alsatian puppy bringing up the rear. She'd run out of free samples and certain elements of the public were distinctly unhappy. Earnest headed off, 200 yards along the main road and back up the hill.

Five thirty. Inside Pat's Quality Fruit & Vegetables he stood behind a raddled-looking woman, lunatic wild hair, white insane frozen face, an empty pushchair. The absent infant situated to the right of the counter. He was immaculately turned out. Pierced ears and an idiot smile, a miniature dark-blue Gola track suit, red wraparound shades. His tousled blonde head pressed hard against a punnet of early-season strawberries.

'What on earth are you doing sonny?'

'I listening to the strawbee-berries mister.'

On impulse Earnest got himself a punnet, avoiding the one the kid had been dribbling into, along with one pound of Spanish onions and four pounds of pre-washed King Edwards. He returned to his dwelling.

Earnest spread out the morning paper on the kitchen table, clicked back the second-biggest blade on his regimental souvenir pocket knife, and the yucca's life story disappeared beneath a translucent drift of King Edward skin.

Six o'clock. Earnest plopped denuded tatties into a saucepan, filled it with cold water, salted it and for now left it at that. There was work to be done.

Upstairs he stripped to his Y-fronts, applied fresh sheets to the bed, erected his second-best set of curtains, engaged in a little light dusting and then set to work on himself.

A sequel to the shave, a second shit and a supplementary shoe-shine. Earnest laid his costume out on the bed, carefully. Very carefully, like his life depended on it. Which it did. Inky black tux, snow-white 100 per cent cotton shirt, midnight-black silk socks, total-eclipse-of-the-sun-black patent shoes, previously polished to an hysterical sheen. Then the final flourish.

Rust-coloured silk shot through with cerise and so soft you'd hardly know you had it on. A bow tie.

It was just like the one Mad Jack wore in the mess when he hit the formal wear on Friday evenings. Exactly like it. It was it. He'd had to bribe that orderly a tidy sum to get it for him but looking at it now gleaming under the pale forty-watt bulb, it had been worth every last penny.

Earnest paused and slid open his sock drawer for a second time. *Why not?* he thought. *Got to keep my spirits up somehow.*

He reached past two rows of socks neatly rolled into pairs, behind them a frilly lavender bag his sister had sent and beside that a black .38 Webley service revolver.

Earnest gently extracted his second most prized possession. Solid silver. Rainbow ribbon with a bronze clip. A medal. He didn't want to talk about it. Anybody would have done that in the line of duty, it was part of the job. Earnest clipped it inside the jacket. She'd never see it but he'd feel better.

Seven o'clock. Downstairs Earnest strapped on a garish PVC apron his sister had sent. It was emblazoned with a large grinning Paddington Bear. Earnest felt a complete chuff in it, but it minimised splashes.

Earnest opened all the tins and lined them up on the drainer. He peeled the onions, chopped the onions, scraped them into a bowl and set it on the drainer alongside the topless tins. He was ready.

Time for a little light music.

The Radfords required at least thirty minutes' warm-up time before performing at anything approaching peak efficiency, but this evening Earnest was in a crazy care-free mood. He poured himself a Harvey's Bristol Cream, sparked up a Senior Service, gave them fifteen minutes and stuck a record on the LP12. He sat down on the green cottage two-seater in the front room.

At this moment Earnest was definitely the only hetero-sexual in the whole of South Yorkshire wearing only Y-fronts and a plastic Paddington pinny. Dressed to kill.

Slim didn't want to hear a love song, all he wanted was the prairie and the open sky. He didn't want to hear a sad story full of heartbreak and desire. Last time he felt like this he was in the wilderness and the canyon was on fire. He stood on the mountain and he watched it burn, watched it burn.

Earnest fought back the tears. It was the army, it was Jack, it was the outside, it was Nella, it was the Harvey's, it was the music.

It's the onions.

Earnest stubbed out a Senior Service, finished the sherry, carried the ashtray back into the kitchen, rinsed it, dried it and held it to the light to check for smears.

Time to get busy.

Earnest put the spuds on full blast. Transferred the

kitchen table to the centre of the front room, spread out a lace cloth his sister had sent and set one stiff-backed chair on either side.

Back in the kitchen he opened the door at the top of the cellar stairs.

A scruffy ginger tabby burst yowling and spitting out of the musty space and clawed his bare leg.

Jesus, how many more times?

Earnest booted it out the back door. He fetched twin candles and a pair of empty Bristol Cream bottles. He inserted a candle into the mouth of each one, set them on the table and sparked them up with his regimental souvenir Zippo.

He checked the spuds, put a big cast-iron frying pan on a low light, melted some butter and shoved in the onions. He felt the rising panic most unreconstructed honest blokes experience when there's more than one pan on the cooker. He had to turn the onions off for a while to let the tatties catch up, then he mashed them, turned the gas on again under the onions and combined the two. Earnest added corned beef, drained the sweetcorn and added that. He whipped it up with a flat wooden spatula, fluffy pink beef-flavoured candy floss with yellow bits in. Ernie's special.

Eight fifteen. Nella knocks the front door. Earnest opens and they smiled.

'Hi Ernie, sorry I'm a bit early but I can smell it next door. It's driving me mad. I'm starving.'

Nella stepped through the front door. Fur, fishnets, boots, no other visible garments.

Shit. No other visible garments.

He'd forgotten the tux. He was wearing less than her.

Earnest dashed upstairs, stood sweating and ashamed in the bedroom. Covered in confusion and not too much else

'Love the apron,' Nella shouted after him. 'What's this greasy paper doing on the mat?'

Nice legs, she thought. *Gorgeous little bum.*

'Sit down and help yourself to a sherry, love,' Earnest shouted back, breaking the all-time, all-comers, all-England record for simultaneously donning evening dress and desperately trying to regain one's composure. 'I'll be with you in two ticks,' he croaked, Mad Jack hysteria in his voice. He slipped Paddington back over the tux and bounded down the stairs.

Two ticks later, Earnest eased Nella out of the fun fur, hung it on the back of the kitchen door, thrashed the pink stuff a bit more, dispensed with the pinny and served up.

'Hey Ernie this is lovely! Looks a bit funny but it tastes wonderful.'

'Just a little something I picked up during the service of Queen and Country. Glad you like it love.'

Halfway through his first mouthful Earnest attempted to come to terms with Nella's outfit. A red satin cap-sleeved blouse so tight it looked like she'd sprayed it on. Breast pockets and twin pearl buttons corresponding exactly with the . . .

. . . where the, where her . . . Blimey!

Black velvet choker and a tiny lime-green vinyl mini.

Red high-heeled PVC boots terminating just above the knees.

Towards the end of the first quarter-pound of the pink stuff, Nella started to notice Earnest's outfit. Silky black tux, crisp white shirt. That bow tie, those silk socks, those gorgeous shiny shoes. A glint of something inside his jacket.

Oh, my word.

Nella made short work of her portion of the pink stuff. Drained the Harvey's. Stood up and jiggled around the table. Settled herself on Earnest's knee. Slipped her hand inside his crisp shirt.

'Hello, love, do I know you?'

'Would you like to Ernie?'

They raced up the stairs.

Five thirty in the morning. Earnest Griffin snapped awake as the central heating kicked in. For the first time in ages, the screams of regimental sergeant-major 'Mad Jack' Harris weren't ringing in his ears. It dawned on him that he wasn't in the army any more.

A shaft of light pierced perfectly clean but threadbare curtains. Earnest could hear her from next door moaning in her sleep. He shifted on to his side, the monster stirring between his legs.

Oh, sweet Jesus.

He could *see* her from next door moaning in her sleep. She rolled over on to his arm.

Blimey, the lovely lady.

Earnest fought back the tears. 'Operation Nella a total success sarh,' he whispered.

He needed the loo but he'd have chewed his arm off rather than disturb her. The tux was a crumpled heap on the floor and he didn't care. There was big black pair of lacy knickers by Deesyr of Tinsley hanging off the bedside lamp. Lying there with his arm going dead, he decided against any cleaning today. Earnest gazed at the undies, tears in his eyes, happier than he could ever remember. Bursting for a piss and listening to the rain.

Amy went through to the front room, got one green bottle from the sideboard, poured herself a nice big sherry, sparked up a Superking and stuck the telly on. Bluff Cove, little grey boats on fire, thick clouds of smoke, helicopters.

Peace. Frank would sleep right through and all the cats were out fighting, shitting and murdering the local fauna. Sleepy little balls of fur by day, cold-blooded psychopaths by night.

Mornings, Amy's kitchen was a grisly Show And Tell. Mice, baby rats, frogs, mangled fledgling birds, shattered koi carp. The dafter ones brought in leaves, earthworms and fluff out of the neighbours' tumble driers. Last week Stanley fetched her half a pizza.

Frank really was going to have to go. It was him or her and she certainly wasn't leaving. It was her house, her job that paid the rent and her name on all the bills.

She'd met him at the doctor's two years ago when Asee, the black doctor, was still practising. Amy trusted Dr Asee implicitly; if he'd told her she had two weeks to live, she'd have died in a fortnight, just to oblige.

Amy there for sleeping tablets, Frank for his cough. They got talking. Ten minutes later they met in the chemist's, got talking again and went to the Arundel for a quick one.

Amy didn't remember when or how Frank had moved in. He'd called round next day, she cooked him his tea and he never went home. She didn't know if he even had a home.

Amy always attracted strays. This time she got one with prison tattoos and a drink problem. This one still had his balls on. Anyway he had to go.

Amy dozes off. One by one the flumps come home, driven in by rain, and settle. Settle on her.

Five thirty in the morning she wakes up with a start. She's wearing a head-to-toe steaming fun fur, and it's alive.

Adeline walked through to Catriona's kitchen, filled the beige plastic Swan kettle from the cold tap, instinctively went to put it on the cooker, remembered just in time and plugged it in. She knew what was happening. She knew Catriona was unhappy and it upset her to think her closest friend couldn't confide in her.

It's just her pride, she thought.

Catriona was ashamed and Adeline understood, but she still wished they could talk about it.

She went into the front room and switched on Catriona's telly. A teak-effect ITT sixteen-inch ex-rental model from Bunker & Pratley. There was a lovely film on this afternoon and she and Catriona were going to watch it: *Seven Brides for Seven Brothers*. They'd both been looking forward to it all week and Catriona had cleaned the house especially.

'Set in the old West, seven hard-working brothers decide they need wives and carry off young women from the villages around,' it said in the paper. It got three stars and was on BBC One, which was even better as there'd be no distracting commercials.

Adeline insisted Catriona sit in the front room while she made the tea. She arranged Fondant Fancies on a willow-pattern plate, set out two china cups, saucers, milk jug and sugar bowl on a Britannia metal tray. The kettle boiled and switched itself off. Adeline hotted the pot, spooned in three good ones and made a nice brew of Co-op Indian Prince all ready for the film.

They settled on the sofa with tea and cakes. The MGM logo appeared on the screen. The opening credits rolled and the story began. For the next 104 minutes Catriona and Adeline were transfixed. Transported to a folksy, Technicolor, lace-trimmed world where the sun was always shining, the neighbours were unfailingly neighbourly and where loving plaid-shirted husbands neither perished needlessly in industrial accidents nor perpetrated malicious practical jokes on their radiant gingham-clad wives.

Elaborate ranch-style letters said 'The End'. The cast list rolled up the screen and the two old girls excitedly discussed the picture, agreeing that Howard Keel was a real looker and the barn-raising sequence was the best bit.

Tom and Jerry came on. Tom was pursuing Jerry around a house, flailing at him with an oversize baseball bat. Adeline got up, quickly as she could manage, and turned off the telly. Catriona seemed so happy now that she couldn't bring herself to mention the bad thing.

I'll do it tomorrow, she thought.

They arranged to meet next morning and go shopping. Adeline said goodbye.

Adeline unlocked her front door, went inside and sat in her own front room. She listened to the early evening news on the radio. The *Sir Galahad* was on fire. She was weary, full of cake and didn't fancy any tea. It had been a lovely day.

She went up to bed.

Catriona heard the front door go and winced. Percy came through to the kitchen, slipped his arm round her waist and she felt her insides shrivel. He smiled and gave his darling wife a kiss. Repington had come in at sixteen to one in the three thirty at Chepstow and Percy was in a very good mood. He sat down at the kitchen table as Catriona put the kettle on.

'What's happened to your face love?' he asked, sounding genuinely concerned.

'I fell down the stairs Percy.'

'Really? Did tha' miss a step?'

'No Percy, I hit every single one and you know why as well.'

'Oh . . . sorry, that were just meant to be a joke. Anyroad, I thought you'd most likely see 'em. Sorry.'

'Look Percy, I know you think it's funny but you could have killed me this afternoon. I want you to stop it. I'm ashamed to leave the house looking like this. It's making me unhappy and God knows what Addy must think.'

'All right love, I'm sorry. I just get a bit carried away. Tha' knows I'm fond of thee really.' He grinned, slipping a drawing pin on to her chair.

Five thirty. Catriona woke up on her front, her face wet with tears. She felt the band-aid on her left buttock sticking to her nightie.

Percy snoring like a natural disaster. No chance of her getting back to sleep now. She jabbed him with her elbow and he started his Yogi Bear impression. The snoring got louder, and Percy added a whistle to the groan. Catriona reached over to the bedside cabinet, then popped a handful of hairgrips into his open mouth.

She swung her legs out of bed, gasped as the soles of her feet made contact with freezing lino, and put her dressing gown on. She went downstairs. Now fully awake, Catriona realised what she'd done. She stood in the 7 × 5 offshot kitchen listening to the noise coming from the 12 × 12 front bedroom. She made a pot of tea and sat at the table gripping her cup tightly, watching the rain, and crying as she waited for her punishment to begin.

Robert Salthouse reached through the shattered pane, wound back the Yale one hundred and eighty degrees, shoved the front door open, staggered through the front room to the offshot kitchen. He rinsed his lacerated arms under the kitchen cold tap. Bloodied water ran down the underneath of his forearms, dripped off his elbows and back into the sink.

It wasn't so bad. He'd avoided the wrists, which was a relief.

Could've been a lot worse anyway.

Robert went back through to the front room and collapsed on to the sofa. He slept.

Five thirty in the morning. Dawn. Raining. Robert sat bolt upright, wasn't sure whether he'd dreamed it or not, looked down at clotted forearms and remembered.

Two inches left in the Teacher's. Robert poured. Pilfered Festival Ale House glass. Sipped. Seconds later his nervous system regained the will to live. Robert felt a lot better, rolled a fag, sparked it up and listened to the rain. He peered through the muck on his front window. The sun breaking through, illuminating the drizzle. Robert heard his mother's voice.

'Come and see, Bobby,' she said softly, then smiled and slipped her arm around his shoulders. 'Sunshine and rain at the same time. It's a monkey's birthday.'

Ken unlocked the front door with his left hand, went through the front room, the back room and into the kitchen. He ran his right hand under the hot tap. Milky white water ran down his arm and dripped on to the floor. He cleaned it up quick before his mum could see and went upstairs. He lay down on his bed.

Two thirty in the morning Ken woke up in his clothes.

Still bored and his mouth dry, he went downstairs to the kitchen and got himself a cola from the fridge. Ken stumbled into the front room, cracked open the can and sat. Nothing on telly now except *Jobfinder* or Bob Fraek from the Open University demonstrating wave formations. Ken flicked through his mum's paper; it was all about gardening.

Ken switched off, put his mum's paper where he'd found it, went into the kitchen, out the back door and across the knackered tarmac yard. Ken let himself into next door with a key he'd pinched on a previous trip. He went through the kitchen, through the back room, into the front room, sat on a creaking sofa and sipped his cola. Across the room Ken noticed something glowing orange. He wandered over.

A small fire dying in the grate. Ken rattled the coals with a poker like he'd seen them do in *Upstairs Downstairs*. The old guy from *The Professionals*, chambermaids getting shagged by the toffs.

It's many a mickle makes a muckle, Mrs Bridges, I'm going to need plenty of hot water, a potato, some blacklead, some clean towels, and all that shit.

Little flames erupted and Ken stretched out on the hearth rug. He watched as the embers began to cool, collapsing in on themselves, orange to red, red to blue, hot white powder to cold grey dust.

An hour later and Ken half awake and half asleep underneath a crocheted bedspread by Catriona c. 1970. By his side an Empire-made glass c. 1960 paid for with Green Shield Stamps containing 250 ml of Dairycrest milk from Netto and four McVities chocolate digestives, also from Netto and weighing approximately 15 g each, on a twelve-inch-diameter blue-and-white striped Cornishware plate by T. G. Green & Co. c. 1933.

So she knows then. It doesn't seem like she's bothered.

He dozed off.

Five twenty-five in the morning Ken snapped awake from a Community-Service nightmare. Glyn had bitten his arm off and Harry and the big-nosed spotty bloke were trying to sew it back on. It was on the wrong way round and they were laughing. The stitches were all on the inside. A taxi came to take Ken to casualty but Glyn had taken the engine out. Blue-green letters on his forehead said 'FUCK YOU KENNY JOBS A GOODUN'. They were all laughing.

The girl was taking a photograph; she knew and she didn't seem bothered. She was laughing. Everybody laughing. It was getting light and everybody was laughing.

Ken didn't remember where he was or how he'd got there, but wherever he was there was somebody else. He could hear them moving about upstairs. The toilet flushing like a huge round of applause, then footsteps on the top landing. He took a shiny cross-shaped thing from the mantel and went to have a look.

Ken crept up the stairs, turned left into the 12 × 12 front bedroom. She was sitting up in bed writing. A marbled notebook. A bronze-coloured fountain pen.

The first blow caught her immediately under the left ear and she made a sound like the last gasp of a clockwork push-and-go toy. She was laughing. Ken hit her a second time and she began a pitiful gurgling noise. Three more blows to the face to the face to the face and she shut up. She was dying but she wasn't going without a struggle and by the time the tenth blow registered there wasn't a face. She still trying to speak, but the lips gone, the jaw smashed and she an earless skull devoid of flesh. Ken covered in blood, Jesus wearing a flesh-coloured headscarf. Rain outside. Ken spotlighted by the sun.

He went back for an encore. Fifteen more blows and there wasn't a skull. Her head pulped and extinct. He folded back the crocheted counterpane.

Five thirty-five in the morning, 16 May 1982. Two days before her ninety-third birthday Ken lost his virginity.

He didn't know why.

English Electric

I shut my eyes and it starts.

A mucky pink dress, scabby knees and scuffed red sandals. I hear screaming and taste smoke. I open my eyes.

I get off the bed, go downstairs and stick the kettle on. I take my mug through to the shed. It's getting light and I've got to make a start. I get my tools, the list and my bag of metal plates. I reckon there's three to do today, but I take them all just in case. Since she left it's public transport or shankses for me. It's going to take a while.

This old street's had it. Worn away, slowed down, furred up and knackered. All my life it's been fading out and today it's finally broken. Seized. Locked up solid. Most of the shops are boarded up or burnt out or both. The only ones doing business are Everything's A Pound. There's still the little baker's on the corner. It's been there since I was a kid. I go in to get a sarnie, so I can smoke without feeling sick. The lady who runs it's two days older than water. Her hands are shaking so badly she can hardly get her fingers in the till. Under the glass-topped counter there's a faded card specked with fly shit. Trembly letters read 'CAKES FOR THE SPECIAL OCCASION'.

Next to it on a paper plate there's an example of the old girl's handiwork.

It's the wrong colour for food, more grey than brown. Halfway down the filling's oozing out like pus from a bedsore. White blackmail-note caps scrawled across the top say LIFE BENIGS AT 40 and she's crammed a stockade of forty candles round the edge. Most of them have been lit before and the cake slumps way off to the right. It looks like a scale model of a mining disaster.

I have to cut through town for the first one. Every second person looks insane. The man ahead of me in the post-office queue bursts into song, then into tears. Outside in the street there's a young couple screaming at each other. Two feet away their son sits roaring in a knackered pushchair, great wicks of snot oozing down his face.

The bus pulls into the station – the Transport Interchange – and I get on. I sit right at the back, as far away from the driver as possible. I'm the only passenger. The bus swings out of the Interchange, up the hill out of town and threads its way past eighties Tory visions of home ownership for all. Lace curtains bunched up like saucy underwear hang at newly installed diamond-leaded UPVC windows. Porcelain figurines, painted by internationally renowned porcelain-figurine painters, gaze out onto shiny Ford Fiestas parked on freshly block-paved driveways. Outposts of neat gentility. Tiny islands of respectability, cut off, then paralysed by the swamp, the biggest, bleakest, most brain-rottingly depressing council estate in Europe.

I get off the bus in the dead centre of the estate. The air tastes of polythene and somebody's smashed a toilet on the footpath. I pick my way through china-studded dogshit and I see two kids crouching in some bushes doing god knows what with carriers and an aerosol. First on the list today is at the tail end of a cul-de-sac about five minutes' walk away.

Chadwick Road. Substation No. 549

A baby this one, and amongst my favourites. Built in the 1930s, massively over-engineered and still going strong, last link in the chain from power station to domestic fuse box.

All the equipment exposed, not bricked up anyway, protected from the elements by curved Morris Minor–style sheet-metal cabinets, painted green and padlocked. A bank of forward-winch Reyrolle circuit breakers connect a flat copper busbar supplying 11,000 volts to a pair of humming oil-cooled transformers which step the power down to 415 volts.

Inside a heavy cast-iron cupboard a low-voltage board carries an array of 400-amp fuses with brass contacts, each one capped with a knobbly white porcelain grip the size of a Cornish pasty. At the base of the cabinet the outgoing cables are tapped through 30-amp cartridge fuse boxes to a timer which controls the streetlamps. Then the cables wriggle down into a pit and slither out under the streets. Next stop is your house.

Back at the bus stop there's a man waiting. Camouflage gear, a swallow on his neck and a blotched purple face. The kind of face that's been in lots of pubs and too many fights. He starts rolling a fag. I unzip my bag, rummage for my baccy tin and begin rolling one myself, first smoke of the day.

Out the corner of my eye I see him spark up and I wonder if he's thinking what I'm thinking. He takes the first drag.

The bus turns up, right on cue. He chucks the fag in the road, gobs, then turns and cracks me a grin.

'Never fucking fails does it pal?'

I was doing all right. I'd worked hard at school. I stayed in most nights studying while my mates were out getting pissed on Strongbow and trying to shag some lass or other. I read books without being told. Used words that got the piss taken out of me. I got decent O levels and went straight into an apprenticeship at Tyzack's.

Tyzack's manufactured tools, everything from sets of screwdrivers right up to agricultural tools – hydraulic fitments for tractors, machine sections for balers, chaff-cutting knives for combines and threshing machines. They set me on a lathe in machine shop number seven, where they made the really big stuff.

By the time they'd taught me to use it, I could scan a blueprint, read off the specs and turn a chunk of steel into something useful. I got to use my brain and my hands. I loved it. I did day release at tech for two years and passed City and Guilds Workshop Practice first time. Five years later Tyzack's made me foreman.

Youngest ever in the history of the firm. I got my photo in the paper.

Once a week the initial plans and specs came down from the drawing office. Me and the technical supervisor scrutinised, picked faults, converted all the metric sizes and tolerances back to imperial so the lads who were fabricating the parts could understand them, then sent the drawings back upstairs again for final approval.

Day to day, my job as foreman meant wandering about with a clipboard, drinking far too much tea and ordering in the right materials to get the stuff made. I missed working with my hands, the satisfaction of making something, but at least I was still with the lads on the shop floor and the money was better. Twice a week I'd take my order dockets up to accounts to have them processed – which is where I met Nichola.

I only asked her out for a bet. She was one of those lasses who acted like they were special, just that little bit better than everybody else, and I didn't think she'd look twice at me. First date we ever had it turned out she had a sense of humour. She let me kiss her.

We married three years later, and six months after that Nichola got her job at Abbey National. In those days Abbey gave cheap mortgages to all their staff. We moved out of our little rented place into a house of our own, just around the corner from my folks, decent shops close by, a good-sized spare room and a tiny garden just big enough for a swing.

I'd go for a pint after work sometimes and talk shit with the lads from Tyzack's. Nichola went out with her mates from Abbey, talked about the royal family, babies, periods or whatever it is women talk about when they get together, and on Saturday mornings we'd both hit B & Q. We'd spend the rest of the weekend Doing It Ourselves. We were respectable. We Got the Habit. We saved for a family car. Nichola started calling the spare room the nursery. We were happy.

Tyzack's closed 12th January 1979 – left it till then so they didn't ruin Christmas. Last week there we pinched anything we could fit under our coats. All the lads took phones, tools, doorknobs, whatever. Me, there was only one thing I really wanted, apart from my fucking job back.

It was such a big works that we had our own electricity substation. A low brick box topped off with a flat concrete roof and two big grey transformers fenced inside a compound. Once every couple of months a man from the Electric called round to inspect it. Usually I'd fetch him a cuppa, and while he unlocked the compound and checked over the equipment, we'd chat.

He'd been working for the Electric all his life. His official title was substation engineer. He had two thousand on his list, ranging from a few real monsters fed straight from the National Grid down to the hundreds of small ones which supplied a handful of streets or a single factory like Tyzack's. He told me about his job, how when the power came in, the substations stepped it down a stage at a time, then filtered it out all over the city. A lethal torrent, harnessed, dammed and diverted, subdued into thousands of tiny streams. I was fascinated.

Tyzack's substation had a sign on it, they all do. A metal plate enamelled bright yellow. Inside a black triangle, a silhouetted man falling backwards, pinned down by a giant cartoon lightning bolt like something out of Tom and Jerry. Across the bottom, black capitals said DANGER OF DEATH, only on ours some clever cunt had scraped away part of the G so DANGER read DANCER.

When the works shut down I thought Right, I'm having that.

I took it home and set it on top of the telly. Nichola thought it was hilarious. She still loved me then.

Back at the bus station I pop into the Snacketeria.

I get myself a coffee, then select a table by the window. The table's bolted to the floor and somebody's carved DARREN FUCKS PIGS into its red Formica surface. I dump my bag of tools by the bench, which is also bolted to the floor, and sit down. Spreading out my list, I cross off Chadwick Road, sip my coffee, which tastes OK, and plan my next visit. The caff smells like a hospital. Disinfectant and sick. Unlike a hospital it's almost empty.

An old girl trundles up to my table. Asks if she can join me. She's having a stainless-steel pot of tea for one and a baked potato with grated cheese on top. This is her little treat. The highlight of her day, her week, who knows, her whole flipping life, and she's going to force a conversation.

She glances at my unzipped bag, sees the tools inside and asks me what I do. I do what any decent man in my situation would do. I lie.

I tell her I'm a plumber. That's all she needs to hear and now she's off on one, moaning about how cold it's been lately, how pensioners don't get enough to live on these days and how she wishes she could afford central heating. Every time she flaps her mouth her top set of dentures winch down into her gob on cheesy saliva strings, and as she munches her spud, they stick back again, each time with a little more slop underneath.

She begins to dribble and starts banging on about the Common Market, how her daughter married a German and they've got four cars and two double garages outside their detached house. I've no time for this today so I bolt the last of my coffee, pick up my bag, say goodbye and get going. She waves me all the way to the door.

The 97 pulls into stand C3. I get on. I pay the man. The bus wallows through town and heads out into a nice bit of suburb. A highly desirable residential area unscathed by strikes or closures. Occasionally the bus pulls over to pick up well-preserved ladies in camel coats and Burberry scarves who've left the car at home today and are doing their bit to protect the environment. Ladies who lunch.

Tree-lined crescents and groves, decent shops, pubs that do dinners and correctly punctuated graffiti. Huge Victorian villas. Places with reception areas, utility rooms and a woman who does. We slide past one, complete with fairy-tale turret, tennis court and a lodge at the entrance to a sweeping gravel drive. These people don't piss around with gardens – they've got grounds.

I get off at the end of an avenue. The bus stop's

immaculate. A shiplap structure which reeks of creosote. Hanging baskets and a notice board for the bridge club. Immediately behind it, down a short tarmac track, is second on the list today.

Montgomery Road. Substation No. 1965

Pretty much the same set-up as Chadwick Road except the equipment's made by South Wales Switchgear. Clipped laurel bushes inside the fence. The land it's on takes a tiny corner out of four different sets of grounds, and four different mansion owners have done their very best to conceal it behind leylandii, climbing roses and trellis.

I crouch down by the fence, unzip my bag and take out a metal plate. A wave of envy smacks into me. If I had all this I wouldn't hide it away. I'd be straight down to B & Q, get myself a set of the biggest garden floodlights money could buy and shine them straight at it. Then I'd wait until dusk, stretch out on my luxury rattan patio set, sip two-hundred-year-old lager from an I Heart Electricity mug and soak up the view, serenaded by the perfect hum of transformers, and dreaming of all that juice blasting out under the streets.

Back in the Snacketeria I get a stainless-steel pot of tea for one and sit at the same table. Darren still Fucks Pigs.

I pour my tea and roll a fag. I can't ever drink tea these days without thinking about work and in particular about Russ. The factory fool. Manufacturing industry's answer to the village idiot.

He'd been there as long as anybody could remember, always the first to turn up in the mornings and the last to go at night. Russ had the mental age of an eight-year-old and, come to think of it, a pretty silly eight-year-old at that. He must have been in his late fifties and he still lived with his mother. Each and every morning she'd pack him off to work with identical butties, a Mars and his little tartan flask. A label sewn inside his coat said who he was and where he lived in case he got lost, and the only thing any of us really knew for certain about Russ was that he liked Elvis. He spent his days sweeping up, running errands and helping out in the dispatch bay, all the shitty jobs they'd give a scheme lad nowadays.

When management decided to enter us in some daft Chamber of Commerce competition for best-kept factory, Russ was given the job of sorting out the tatty flower beds carved out of the knackered turf in front of the admin block.

He picked up all the litter, dug the beds over and planted them out with bulbs. Contractors were hired in to lay fresh turf.

Russ spent a carefree afternoon leaning on his spade, watching as they laid a level bed of sand, then rolled out the turves and tamped them down flat.

Eight o'clock the following morning we clocked in and found Russ sitting in his garden. It looked like a beach. He'd rolled all the turf back up again, stacked it in a neat pile by the entrance, then dug out all the bulbs to see if they were growing. They slabbed it after that.

The best thing about Russ was his teeth. They were

shagged. I saw two fall out as he ate his sarnies one breaktime. He scooped them up, put them in his pocket – probably with all the rest – and carried on munching. He finished up with just the one tooth in the middle, top and bottom. We used to joke about him having central eating.

When the last two dropped out, Russ's ma got him fitted up for a set of falsies. He came to work one morning waving a note, which he made us all read, bus money and a map.

Today was the big day. The day Russ got his new gob.

Twelve thirty. Russ left the factory at the double, hopped on a bus and zoomed off into town.

One fifteen. He was back and smiling like a horse.

Three o'clock tea break. Russ poured himself a nice hot cup of tea. He took a big gulp and his new dentures started to run down his face – pink goo with white chunks, dripping off his chin and pouring down his overalls.

We held him down till he stopped screaming, then peeled a bit of the pink stuff off his front. Wax.

He'd marched into the dentists, got so excited he'd grabbed the first thing he saw, bunged a full-size model of some other bugger's mouth into his stupid face and marched out again.

I finish my fag and knock back the rest of the tea. Last on the list today is a monster, a really fucking big one.

Back on the bus again and heading through an ex-industrial area. The road very straight with huge factories towering up like the walls of a canyon. All the empty works padlocked, patrolled day and night by security firms. Late-middle-aged men – some my mates from Tyzack's – dressed up in pathetic Boys' Brigade uniforms, working long unsociable hours for lousy pay. Gutted by failure and bored shitless.

Further along the road, the factories are already being converted. Ripped apart from the inside, sand-blasted, fitted with red toytown window frames, then put up for sale as office space that nobody needs.

I get off at a stop in front of a memorial, the names of all the steel workers who pegged it in World War I listed on a bronze plaque fixed to the remains of the same factory where it was cast. I fetch a wad of steel wool from my tool bag and shine up grandad.

Attercliffe Grid Station

132,000 volts coming straight off the National Grid via an overhead pylon.

Inside a separate compound, a set of sealing ends, each crowned with big ceramic insulators and tapped to neutral earth resistors – huge tanks of distilled water – feed the power through live copper bars to a step-down transformer. The bars sparking and crackling with static in the damp atmosphere. The transformer is oil-cooled with thermostatically controlled fans as backup. It's the size of a terraced house.

The baby ones hum. This fucker thunders.

There's no chance of me getting in here. It's surrounded by tall spiked railings with an electric fence inside that. I wouldn't want to anyway, it scares the shit out of me.

I bolt my plate to the fence, then go home.

First Monday morning after Tyzack's went down the toilet I woke, washed, shaved, got dressed as usual and was halfway out the front door before I remembered.

It felt like start of the school holidays all over again. I sat in the kitchen – tea, newspaper and fag as Nichola fussed about, then left for Abbey. After she'd gone I switched on the telly and thought this is the life. I still had all my redundancy money then. I felt like lord of the manor. Lunchtime, I met up with a couple of mates who'd also become gentlemen of leisure and we had a few pints. Tuesday was the same. Come Wednesday teatime I was bored out my flaming skull.

Thursday, thought I'd start on the spare room. Time on my hands and all that. I cleared out all the empty boxes and tea chests, then pulled the paper off. Horrible thirties stuff, garish crinoline ladies, half-timbered thatched cottages, gaudy wallflowers, oversized bluebirds. Ye Olde Merrie England.

Nichola came back, asked me what did I think I was doing? No chance of that for a good long while, she said. No point. Kids cost money. She bustled out. Snapped the latch to on the lavvy door.

I always hated it when she cried.

I went out with Nichola Friday night. I'd not worked all week but it still felt like, you know, Friday Night. She gave me a right talking-to. Said she didn't want a husband who sat in the pub all day. Told me I'd better sort myself out pronto or there'd be trouble, said she'd already spoken to my folks and they were very worried about me. I wouldn't have minded but it'd only been a week.

Next day Nichola finally lost her sense of humour. Acting like Little Miss Snippy Knickers. She cold and efficient. Me a complete idiot. Daggers in her eyes, a very sharp knife in her voice, and long lists of stuff for me to do if I could possibly find the time, fit it into my busy schedule.

Monday morning Nichola took the bus to work and left me the car. I drove into town and signed on – first time in my life and I felt like shit. They took my details, told me I wasn't entitled to anything because of Nichola's income and my pay-off. They asked if I'd considered security work, then gave me a phone number and wished me luck.

I dialled the number from a call box. It turned out that there were jobs available at – you've guessed it – Tyzack's. I went up there, just out of curiosity really, and found the old place fenced off, a JCB charging around inside. A brand-new Portakabin at the gate, all the windows wide open. 'Jailhouse Rock' blasting out.

As I pulled in, a man appeared in the doorway. He was wearing a fake policeman's uniform and a white idiot smile.

It was Russ.

On the way home I passed a substation. The standard

low brick box with louvred double doors and a flat concrete roof, surrounded by a tall iron fence. The gate was hanging open. I parked up, wandered in and yanked the sign off.

As a boy I'd always been afraid of substations. Had it drummed into me they were dangerous. Places where bad things happened. My folks told me stories. Kids who went in after kites or footballs and were never seen again. If I saw a substation I'd cross the street to avoid it, not even look at it, so to actually go inside one now, and take something, gave me a real thrill.

I fetched the sign home. Stuck it on top of the telly next to the other one. Nichola got back from Abbey. Told me to get rid of it.

I took it into the shed. That was the real start of my collection.

I jolt awake. The couple next door rowing, shagging, then rowing again. I pull the covers over my head. Try to get back to sleep. Each time I start to nod off they're at it again. Eventually I give up, go to the bathroom, clump downstairs and stick the kettle on.

I take my mug through to the shed. I get my tools and the signs and consult my list; they're all local today. I smoke a quick fag and get going.

It's sunny out but freezing. Suddenly I'm busting for a pee. Apart from that I feel OK. I've got twenty quid in my pocket, a new pack of tobacco and something to do. I really miss Nichola, and I know I can't ever undo what's happened, that putting the signs back won't change anything, but at least this way I'm out of the house and busy. All I ever wanted from a job in the first place.

Albany Road. Substation No. 375

First one today is a bit unusual. The normal brick box, but not fenced off. Plonked on a grassy peninsula at a Y-junction in the road. The station's at the widest point of the Y and at the neck there's a red-brick public toilet which joins on to it. I tighten the last nut and go into the gents'. They do say water and electricity don't mix but this is ideal.

Lunchtime. I'm dying for a pee again. The only places you can go for one round here are the pubs and they get snotty if you don't buy a drink. I head straight for the nearest. It's a big fifties place with a car park, a family beer garden and a games room. The kind of boozer that does Bingo and a Turn at the weekends. I go into the lounge.

The place is covered with red plush, anaglypta and horse brasses except for the actual bar itself which looks like it's been inspired by a Spanish package deal. I order a half and leave the right money on the counter while I go to the gents'.

Back in the lounge, I take the half over to an alcove and flop down. Pain whacks up my spine. The seats look soft in here, but they feel like concrete.

I roll myself a fag and spark it up. There's the odd time when the novelty of not having a job still appeals. This is definitely one of them. I sip the half and take a look around. There're a fair few blokes my age in here for an early weekday morning, which I suppose is typical of this area now, and the odd pensioner – most likely in to keep warm.

When I've finished the half I need a piss again. I go and have one, then get myself a pint. Nichola said she didn't want a man who sat in the pub all day but she's gone now – so who cares?

Pint number three. Nobody's come in, nobody's gone out. Seems like we're all stuck in here for the duration, pissing the day up the wall.

Pint number four. While I'm at the bar, a bloke I only knew by sight at Tyzack's emerges from the games room. We greet each other like old mates and he comes over to sit with me. He glances at the tool bag and asks me if I'm working. I tell him not. We leave it at that.

Reminiscing about Tyzack's like it was some fantastic holiday-camp-cum-public-school, we get on to Russ. I tell him Russ is still there, the only one of us left. Sat day after day in a sweaty hut parked on the remains of his little garden, with only a new set of teeth and his Elvis tapes for company. We have a laugh about that and he goes off to get the pints in. While he's at the bar it dawns on me I'm just as fucking sad. Worse. He's the first person I've spoken to in almost two weeks.

At least Russ has his mum. My folks don't answer the door to me.

The lights flick on. Four o'clock already. How time flies when you're getting leathered. We sink a few more and he asks about the tool bag again. I'm pissed enough to tell him now, to tell him the truth; I want to tell him the truth, but I mutter something about a mate's car instead and change the subject. We drink up and say goodbye.

I stagger home, just make it through the front door, then throw up all over the living-room carpet. I crawl upstairs and into bed with my shoes on, over the fence with a wooden ladder, down the other side on a fibreglass pole, creep across the rose garden and run screaming along a narrow corridor encrusted with glimmering dials and arcing switches.

A semicircular control room. The Grid Station. Attercliffe. Huge green Vitriolite panels map out the nerve system of the city, every substation named, mapped, pinpointed and quantified. Lightning Risk Levels One, Two and Three.

I enter a vast windowless room, an echoing hollow chamber throbbing with power, pulsing like a monster electromechanical heart. The air seethes with energy and I feel my body crackling with fear. The circuit breakers in here are the size of midiskips, the cables thick as telegraph poles, the busbars heavier than a family car.

I walk into the compound, calmer now, acting like I own the place. It's misty and I can't quite see the top of the first set of sealing ends. The noise is unbelievable. I settle on a concrete wedge bearing a yellow danger sign and roll a fag. Nichola sits beside me. I wish you wouldn't smoke in the house she says and I see a blue halo slide along the first of a set of ten copper HT bars. One by one they all do it. Ten HT bars wrapped in a blue ring of confidence, an inverted gas burner edgeways on and the air thundering with power. Nichola slips her arm around my shoulder. We kiss.

I notice a smouldering pink rag sticking out the LV cupboard. An overpowering smell of bacon. I wake up in my clothes. I feel like shit.

I go downstairs and stick the kettle on. I take my mug through to the shed, remember and go back into the house. I open the door to the living room. The stench of rancid beer washes over me. There's sick everywhere. It takes me nearly an hour to clean it all up, then I'm ready to go. Instead I sit down on the sofa, the only thing Nichola didn't take. I roll a ciggy.

It was never the signs, they're all the same. Not the list, the electric, the buzz of not getting caught, or the fucking things piling up in the shed.

I had a purpose, a plan. Little trips out with my bag of tools spinning out my useless fag end of a life. A routine. A way to stop the boredom chewing into my brains. Something to keep my fingers busy.

I feel like it was my fault. I know it wasn't really my fault but I feel like it was. I should have done something, told somebody.

I met the girl on a scruffy bit of grass behind the post office. A nice-looking kid with big brown eyes and curly black hair. Pink clothes from head to toe. I suppose she must've been six or seven. She was dressed as Barbie.

She asked, what I was up to mister?

I said I worked for the Electric and I was taking the sign away to have it mended.

She asked me where did it come from, the electric? And when it went in the big pipes under the ground, could it spill out and hurt the animals that lived in the dirt – rabbits and moles, worms and that?

I said not.

She asked me was it true Jesus died on a hot-cross bun?

The day after, and miles away, she turned up again. She was filthy. I asked her what she was doing. She said she was having an adventure.

Next time I saw her was on the news. She'd been burnt to death.

I pick up my tool bag from the living-room floor where I dropped it last night.

I walk over to Shirland Lane.

Shirland Lane. Substation No. 3009

A brand-new spiked fence with three big yellow danger signs. I bolt mine back with the others. A mountain of rotting flowers. This is where it happened.

I'd visited this one a couple of days before the accident – which is where I first met the Barbie girl – and it was open. Kids break in sometimes to keep warm, smoke fags, drink cider. They'd pulled the door off the LV cupboard.

I should have reported it, taken two minutes away from my stupid list, my pathetic substitute for a job, a life, and I might have saved her, but I didn't.

Two days later she wandered in. The poor little sod fell against the contacts.

Me and Nichola were sat watching the news. By this time I was meant to be working days as a security guard at Tyzack's – just till something decent turned up – but I wasn't. I was out every day with my tools and the fucking list.

The little girl's picture flashed on to the screen. There was a report on the accident. Ashen-faced residents saying how dreadful it was, how when it happened all the power went off, and a woman from the Electric saying there'd be a full inquiry.

They stuck a camera in the mother's face. Asked her how she felt. She went berserk.

Nichola stood up, took the sign off the telly, walked through to the kitchen and slammed the door.

I went in after her. Found her bent over the sink, elbows on the drainer. The sign pressed to her forehead. Tears streaming on to the dirty pots. I put my arms round her, kissed the back of her neck. As my lips touched, she spun round, and with make-up climbing down her face, Nichola slashed at me with the sign. In all she must've hit me twenty or thirty times before she ran out of steam. I stood there taking it and waiting for her to stop. Each blow felt like the end of something, as if Nichola was driving nails back into one of the tea chests in the spare room, packing up what little was left between us all ready for the binmen.

Next day I went into town, drew all my redundancy money out the bank and put it in an envelope.

I took a bus to the estate. I found the house, no

problem. It was close by Shirland Lane Substation and easy to spot. The ruched lacy curtains shut tight and the front garden piled high with flowers – bouquets, wreaths and a giant Barbie made from pink and white carnations. I picked my way up the block-paved driveway and shoved the envelope through the letterbox.

When Nichola got back from Abbey I told her everything. Promised I'd put all the signs back. Nichola knew about them anyway. Said she'd seen them piled up in the shed and guessed I wasn't working.

She left me.

Three to go. Two I missed out yesterday and DANCER OF DEATH.

I get the bus up to Tyzack's. The gate's wide open. It's gone. Bulldozed flat. Nothing left except the substation, and they're knocking that down. I watch through the fence as demolition men forklift big grey English Electric transformers on to a low loader.

A JCB moves in, smashes up the concrete base, then digs a massive pit for all the rubble.

Russ appears in the doorway of the Portakabin. He's waving a teapot. Everybody knocks off and goes inside.

Tyzack's, Little London Road. Substation No. 1849

I go in through the gate, stumbling across broken concrete. I drop my stuff and stand in the shattered guts of substation No. 1849.

Silence.

The air tastes of diesel. I feel alone and useless.

'Return to Sender' erupts from Russ's Portakabin. I pick up my tool bag, my list and the last three signs. Then I chuck the fuckers into the pit.

Early Doors

Bad hair, bad skin, bad breath, bad teeth, bad dandruff. Cyril wasn't exactly everybody's idea of a pussy magnet.

He always sat at the bar. His giant arse folded over a stool and his multi-chin cupped into his stubby mitt, holding forth to anybody bored enough to listen about the Kikes, the Micks, the Poles, the Lesbians, the Homos, the Kids, anyone who drank wine and drove a foreign car, the people who worked at the City Farm, the Council, the Government, the Social Workers, the Health Service, the Unions, the Common Market, the Pakis, the Krauts, the Aytyies, the Arabs, the Gypsies and the Spice Girls. Invariably the only decent-looking woman in the place would stand just that little bit closer than necessary and strike up a conversation.

Cyril's secret was his technique. And his beautiful personality. He'd look them up and down, check out the arse, the tits, the face, in that order, then say 'All right, love, fancy going halves on a bastard?' Generally they did.

Daytimes Cyril was a liar. You name it, he'd sold it. Wigs that made you look stupid, security systems which didn't secure, double glazing that leaked, revolutionary new paint processes which were useless, pans that stuck, mops that didn't mop, dusters which fell to bits and insurance.

Cyril's idea of a good night out was seventeen pints of Castlemaine, six bags of nuts, a take-out and a shag. Then he met Dawn.

Dawn was an ex-Goth. Her new favourite band was M. People. While they were busy promoting their new super-duper disc – Snake Davis doing Sax Masterclass on BBC 2, the drummer camping it up on Channel Five pop quiz shows, and Heather Small sounding increasingly like Kermit The Frog reaming out a rich vein of soft rock, guesting on No-Celebrity Name That Stain – Dawn spent her leisure time collecting pictures of penguins and fiddling with herself, waiting patiently for their next CD to come out.

She'd gone right off Fields of the Nephelim, but she still wore all the gear. When Cyril first laid eyes on her she was sporting black leather pants with eyelets up the sides, laced with red ribbon from ankle to arse, a green vinyl basque, no underwear, and a thick layer of bomb-proof slap. She had hair the texture of cheap noodles six months past their sell-by, fantastic bazooka-joe tits and dark pit-bull eyes.

Cyril took one look and asked her what she was drinking. Dawn named her poison and six 'penis coladas' later Cyril dragged her back to his place, showed her his hi-fi, his fish tank, his mug tree, his kung-fu posters and his collection of Cappa de Monte, then grabbed her tight leather bum and bundled it on to his kink-sized mattress almost paid for on interest-free credit from Sunwin

House. Cyril unlaced pants, extracted tits from plastic container and fucked Dawn every which way but loose, starring Clint Eastwood and a monkey, which was his favourite film.

Next morning Dawn woke up first. Wriggled out from under the beast, rinsed Cyril spunk out her cunt, her arse, her hair, her mouth, her armpits, and went down to the kitchen. Opened the fridge and found the necessary. Brought Cyril up a lovely breakfast.

Full English heart-attack special – free trip to hospital with every complete meal consumed. Cyril bit into the first perfectly cooked Cumberland sausage and fell in love.

Dawn worked shifts at Happy Eater. She wasn't happy and not really that much of an eater. Her diet consisted solely of fresh Diet Coke and stale non-diet fries. Every time she took a break she'd force in a couple of portions of the fries, wash them down with a Coke, then rush straight into the bogs and chuck the whole lot back up again.

Dawn always felt better with her uniform on. It made her look like everybody else, the same reason she'd started dressing Goth in the first place. She looked such a freak she could easily reduce your average building site to stunned silence in five seconds flat.

One by one all her mates had got crappy jobs data-inputting at Midland Bank or Abbey National. They'd stopped dying their hair with Indian ink, gluing bits of carpet to their scalps and backcombing their locks over it for bulk, stopped soaking themselves in petuli oil and hardly ever pretended to be vampire bats who shopped in Sainsbury's anymore.

Dawn had never bothered to stop. There was no need and she'd got dead good at doing the make-up. She painted butterflies on her cheeks, drew spiders on her shoulders, stencilled 666 on her arse, and squirted on so much sugar solution and hairspray that once every three months her fringe fell off.

While Dawn's mates had to console themselves with pathetic little ponytails tied up with black velvet ribbon, settle for tacky skull-and-crossbones jewellery and maybe, just as a treat, a leather bike jacket over a Dead Girls Never Say No T-shirt as they cruised the garden centres for concrete goblins and dead plants at the weekends, Dawn flounced around the Goth emporiums, the sex shops and the hand-crafted crap markets looking like Carmen Miranda dug up, made up, pissed up and back from the dead.

As they drove their clapped-out little Hondas home from work, making machine-gun noises at the pedestrians, no-sell-out, post-sell-by Dawn was still emphatically the real thing. A souvenir and a mascot all rolled into one. Shock to nostalgia without even trying.

Dawn flicked back the duvet, sucked Cyril off, then left for work. Cyril got up at eleven, shaved, shat, showered in his self-installed en suite which leaked like a sieve, went out and sold half a dozen pensioners time shares on a Greek island which didn't exist, then phoned Dawn's work number on his mobile.

Three o'clock, they met up in the Shakey, downed five quick ones and headed back to her place.

Dawn's flat was an unnatural disaster. She'd dispensed with her old suite covered with barbed wire and binliners, the spray-on cobwebs, the inverted crucifixes and the big plastic skulls with snakes crawling out the top, which were just *so* last year, and decided on something altogether more sophisticated and a lot less tasteful. Black ash units, powder-blue walls, thick red shag pile, a pouting pumped-up mushroom leather suite and everywhere framed pictures of penguins. Penguins in the water, penguins out of the water, penguins half in and half out of the water, penguins with their tits out, penguins shagging, penguins laying eggs, penguins having a shit, penguins jumping about on icebergs, and baby penguins getting big red chunks bitten out of them by killer whales. It wasn't cheap and it wasn't cheerful. But it was tidy. Very, very tidy.

Cyril was dead impressed, he asked her to marry him on the spot. Dawn said yes – he wasn't right but he was raw material.

The wedding was a cracker. Dawn wore fluffy red moonboots and a white vinyl number which began at the first curve of her arse and concluded just above the nipples. She didn't blush once, but when they were introduced to Dawn, most of the guests did. Cyril wore a black suit two sizes too small, a brown polyester shirt and an orange bow tie which made him look like Psychotic Noddy. He spent the entire ceremony fighting back a tear in his eye and the lump in his trousers. He drove Dawn to the reception in his multiple-personality Rover 3500 spruced up and all decked out for the big day. It'd had eighteen different registrations and so many resprays it was half an inch bigger than the standard production model.

Cyril stretched pink supersoft bog roll from wipers to radiator grill and lettered I LUV YOU DAWN down it with thick green marker pen.

They held the reception at the Shakey. Dave the landlord took care of the catering; he laid on a sausage roll, two pork pies and gallons of beer.

The £25 a head entrance money which Cyril charged the imaginary Greek time-share owners freezing to death in their newly insulated paint-blistered homes, the housewives who spent five hours a day trying to suck bits of shattered duster off their carpets with faulty vacuums, and the girls and boys who turned up in badly fitting fright wigs, easily paid for everything. In fact the groom made a bit of a profit. The locals got in for free and lolled around the bar leering at Dawn's tits, telling the truth about Cyril and taking bets on how long the marriage would last.

After no more stretcher bearers were required to dispose of the paying guests and the last of the ambulances had faded into the night, the regulars got down to some serious boozing. For a bet Cyril necked a bottle of tequila and the party really livened up.

He had a theory. It was a theory that was all his and it made absolutely no sense. He'd been unpacking a consignment of useless vacuums in his lock-up; they were festooned with yards and yards of bubble pack and he'd come up with the brilliant idea that all the homeless really needed was a great big wad of the stuff and they'd be OK. He added that anybody who was black, homosexual or both and also homeless should be killed and not allowed to have the bubble pack in the first place.

After an hour of Cyril's bubble-pack-for-the-homeless theory Dawn stood up. She cleared her throat and focused on Cyril.

'That is easily the stupidest thing I have ever, ever heard anybody say. Apologise, then shut up.'

Cyril apologised. He shut up. Most of the money that had changed hands earlier – bet on the marriage not lasting – changed back. It seemed like they were entirely suited.

Four thirty in the morning the drinks ran out. Cyril phoned a taxi from the Shakey. An hour later it pulled up, honked, kick-started the dawn chorus and woke all residents within a 500-yard radius. The happy couple fell into the back of a black FX4 and headed back to the bridal suite. Dawn joined in with the chorus and honked on the seat. When they got to Dawn's flat, the driver asked Cyril for a tip.

'Yeah, I've got a right tip for you, yer paki cunt,' he said wittily. 'Clean this fucking seat up.'

Dawn puked again – this time all up the grill where they take the money, which at least filtered out most of the bits.

Marriage number three was a completely new departure for Cyril. There was an element of honesty. It was the first one where he hadn't pretended to be from Tacoma, a town in America where the bridge nicknamed Gurtie galloped itself to pieces in high winds and fell into the Narrows. Cyril really had been there, back in the seventies on a two-week fly-drive bargain break, and he'd found the accent easier to deal with than his own. Plus he'd discovered it created more openings, business and legwise, especially on sales trips down South, and he ended up using it so often he felt comfier talking Yank than Tyke.

Cyril decided to drop the 'I'm from Tacoma' crap with Dawn, third time lucky and all that. Occasionally he'd slip into 'hey there little lady' mode, which made her giggle, but on the whole he was Cyril from Sheffield and it saved a lot of bother.

His first wife Linda, who had sincerely believed he was an American, got far too interested, started asking him about his family and subjected Cyril to a daily general knowledge and fascinating facts quizathon about the States. Most of the time he coped, but when she asked him what the DC stood for in Washington DC he had no idea. Direct Current, Dark Chocolate, Double Chin, Duvet Cover? Daft Cyril didn't have a clue and he'd had to make up a story about his time with the FBI to shut her up. Linda asked him what FBI stood for and he didn't know that one either, so he told her Fancy Barstools International and pissed off down the pub quick as his fat boy insoles would carry him.

Night after the wedding the honeymooners hit a different pub, the bride still wearing the same outfit.

The Cross Guns; seriously violent clientele, gigantic TV, Misty in Roots on the jukebox and a competition-size pool table. Cyril hadn't settled his bill at the Shakey, deciding instead to invest all the takings in an extensive range of German cookware, guaranteed for 'your entire lifetime' and endorsed by Paul Newman.

Cyril asked if Dawn fancied a game, if she wanted to spread his balls out on the table, get hold of his stick etc. – all his usual charming lines. He put a quid in the pool table, racked 'em up and let the lady serve.

Cyril had always fancied himself as Paul Newman, but after Dawn potted all her yellows, then the black, without him getting a touch six times on the trot, he began to lose heart.

A man approached the table. Too much jewellery, white shoes, and a hairdo benefiting from a whole consignment of Grecian 2000. He informed Cyril that the Cross Guns was not and never would be an equal-opportunities pub and fetched a long black case stamped with gold initials from behind the bar. The cunt had his own cue.

Dawn thrashed him three times. A crowd began to gather. The psychos watching repeats of pro-celebrity farm accidents on wide-screen cable TV suddenly lost interest in Tarby and Brucie and gathered round the table to watch Dawn grinding down Mr Jewellery instead.

The crowd was split fifty/fifty. Dawn vs. the Cunt was definitely a game of two halves, half electing to stand behind Dawn and catch a glimpse of her arse each time she bent over to play a shot, and the other lot preferring to face her head-on for a generous measure of tit.

This involved a fair bit of walking as the game moved up and down the table, and Dawn found herself at the centre of a human merry-go-round, a whirling carousel of perves circling the table, bobbing up and down, craning their necks and all the while trying to cop the ultimate eyeful.

When Dawn beat the Cunt again Cyril started taking bets. Two hours later she was four hundred quid up. Dawn was obviously the better player, but for the punters the idea of betting on some bird over a man with that much jewellery and his own cue was a non-starter. They lost heavily.

Dawn got cocky, started taking the piss, played with her eyes shut to give the poor fucker a chance, and when she still won the Cunt went nut-nut. The crowd got ugly and the happy couple withdrew to the bride's place.

Cyril laid all the cash out on the bed just like in *Indecent Proposal* starring Demi Moore, Woody Harrelson and Robert Redford, which was his second-favourite film, stripped Dawn off, spread her out on top of the notes and loose change, unzipped himself and climbed aboard. Five minutes later Cyril really came into some money.

Dawn woke, scraped pennies from her eyes, peeled a soggy fiver off her arse, put her uniform on, didn't make any tea and went straight to work. The honeymoon was over and she was knackered.

Cyril rose at midday, bundled cash into a flesh-coloured plastic carrier, trudged down the brown-carpeted communal stairway, eased out of the front door and fell arse over tit on a loose paving slab in the street. He picked himself up and headed home. He had plans to make and pans to sell. As the multiple-personality Rover chugged painfully up the hill back to his place, Cyril started to get a tingle, a soft shooting ache travelling up through his rectum, spinning out into the pit of his stomach and flooding into his joints. He could feel a lie coming on.

Cyril pushed open his front door, jamming the drift of final demands and court summonses up against the passageway wall, went through to his front room, stuck 'Bring Your Daughter to the Slaughter' by Russ Abbot on the stereo which was his favourite record, poured himself a Malibu, sipped and sat. He needed to think.

Cyril sank into his knackered sofa, sticky coconut-flavoured sludge crawling down his gullet, Russ Abbot fading away on the stereo, the damp rising inexorably up the walls and somewhere across town his new wife chucking it up into a Happy Eater bog. Cyril wedged his mobile into the folds of his multi-chin and phoned Television Ray. Ray was the master, Cyril's hero. He had a twelve-bedroom house in Essex, six acres of land, a top-of-the-range Range Rover, a beautiful wife, a matching pair of au pairs, three grey greyhounds and a duckpond with some ducks in it.

The phone rang for ages before Ray picked up. He

was stretched out on a beige leather La-Z-boy in his lounge, David Bowie's version of 'I've Got My Beer in the Sideboard 'Ere' blasting out of his gold-plated midi system and in the pond five hundred yards away a pair of mallards joining in. The room was the size of a bowling alley, polystyrene Jacobean beams, fake horse brasses and *The Hay Wain* bolted round the place at random. Ray was wearing a black silk dressing gown with red Chinese characters screen-printed on the back, which he didn't know translated as Lucky VD Clinic. He spoke into a phone which was mostly gold paint and fake green onyx. It looked like a dodgy shower attachment.

'All right there, me old mukka? Sorry about the delay, the wife's chasing the bleeding ducks again. Didn't recognise the voice without the Yank at first Cyril. So, what can I do you for?'

'I got wed again, two days ago. Her name's Dawn and –'

'So where was my invite then, you soppy minge? Lost in the bleedin' post, I don't think?'

'Sorry Ray, there wasn't time. She's the best ever. I had to get it done before she changed her mind. Anyway, I need your help.'

'Sure, Cyree. As the bard said, Love is as blind as a many splendoured thing – so I take it she has changed her mind?'

'No Ray, I need some business advice. Remember years back when we were both repping?'

'Err, nope . . . Yeah, sure. Sorry mate, the wife's tormenting the greyhounds now, can't think straight.

'Leave 'em alone, darlin', there's plenty of gear in the freezer. They'd be too stringy anyway.

'Sorry about that Cyril. Right, you have my undivided attention. How can I help you chief?'

Before Cyril could tell him the signal faded. Cyril's mobile packed up, and he sat alone and hopeless in his grotty front room. The electricity conked out, the heads fell off his entire collection of Cappa de Monte, the sun went down, all the weeds in his garden wilted, it started to rain, and corner by corner the Blu-Tack died on the backs of his kung-fu posters. One by one they fluttered to the floor, exposing stark white patches of nicotine-free anaglypta.

Then Cyril cracked it. It stopped raining and got light again, the power came back on and he came up with his own plan – and without any help from that cockney git Raymond either. Cyril fixed himself a further Malibu and relaxed. He slept.

Dawn breasted double swing doors, pushed aside a slatted polythene curtain, tripped over a loose floor tile and stumbled into the food-preparation area. She hung her coat in a narrow steel locker, crammed a white mesh trilby over her rigid back-combed hairdo and got herself a tea-flavoured beverage from the staff machine. The man who'd installed it had fucked up bigtime. Dawn wedged her arse against the antiseptically clean work surface and sipped. She got a hint of coffee, 2 per cent tomato soup, 20 per cent Bovril, 7 per cent hot still orange, 10 per cent P.G. Tips, and 61 per cent stagnant water. It tasted like shit. The first 20 ml of the stuff hit the pit of her stomach, bottomed out, and Dawn leaned over the nearest big aluminium double sink and vommed it back up.

The punters flooded in. Sporting matching trainers and unusual skin conditions, they troughed happy breakfasts, maudlin brunches and overindulged on unsupervised supersized unhappy meals.

Dawn's shift ended at two but by eleven-thirty breaktime she could hardly keep her eyes open and when she threw herself onto the greasy vinyl settee in the staffroom she began to cry. Dawn put twenty pence in the payphone and dialled her own number. Nothing. He'd either gone home or he was still asleep.

Two o'clock. Dawn shoved her hat in the locker, pulled on her coat and left. She walked to the bus stop in the rain. The bus surged past without stopping so she blew two hours' wages on a cab to get her home. Dawn pushed open the front door, staggered up the brown-carpeted communal stairway, unlocked the door to her flat, kicked off her shoes, flopped down on to her king-sized black satin-sheeted bed spattered with Cyril spunk and wept. She felt dirty, tired and sore. She'd just married an older man she knew next to nothing about and she was still hoping to fall in love.

Cyril woke with a start and felt tepid white Malibu running down his fat pink legs and congealing into the heel sections of his kicked-out grey slip-ons. He stood up, squelched across crumpled posters, went out the front door, crossed his withered garden, squigged out into the street and shoved a quid in the nearest pay-phone.

It rang and rang and rang and rang and rang and rang, then Dawn picked up. Half an hour later they were together in the Shakey and right after he'd settled his bill Cyril made a short speech. Confessed how much he loved her, mentioned how he was a cunt, a con-man, a liar, a thief and ten years older than he'd said. Cyril said that he loved her properly, like in the films and everything, and what with her being his wife now and all, would she like to move in with him, help him tidy up and maybe go Dutch on the rent? Dawn said yes and burst into tears.

Next morning Dawn phoned in a sicky, collected cardboard boxes from Pat's Quality Fruit & Vegetables, packed selected items of her stuff, abandoned the rest, and flitted. By mid-afternoon she'd installed herself at Cyril's and ordered a skip.

Cyril got back at teatime – exhausted and only slightly richer after a hard day's cold-calling – and thought he'd been turned over. The front room bare, except for the European single-market middle-of-the-floor bin-liner mountain, and the back parlour completely empty. Cyril found Dawn on her hands and knees in the kitchen scrubbing furiously at a black and yellow chequerboard lino floor which he'd always assumed was just a black lino floor. The mountain was Cyril's stuff bagged up all ready for the skip and he had to beg Dawn not to sling the truncated Cappa de Monte. Twenty minutes later they reached a compromise. The kind of thing married life is all about. She let him keep the heads.

Cyril pulled into a Texaco, put as much petrol into the Rover as it would take and drove off without paying. He checked his reflection in the rear-view mirror. Good hair, good teeth, greatly improved skin and spiffy new clothes. He looked ten years younger.

Cyril felt Dawn's hand on his leg, turned and grinned at his wife. She looked fantastic. Short black bob, even shorter black leather skirt, tiny red top, designer sunglasses. Two months into the marriage and it was going great. His wife was gorgeous, his house was clean, his hair was clean, his teeth were clean, even his socks were clean. These days the only dirty thing about Cyril was his mind.

Cyril eased back a crisp cotton cuff and glanced at his brand-new watch.

Eleven thirty – plenty of time yet. He decided on the scenic route.

Twelve thirty. The Rover chugged into a village. Six thatched cottages – all with Range Rovers parked outside – a pond, a post office and a pub. Cyril parked up and they went inside.

The view from the beer garden of the Barley Mow was nature. It was fucking everywhere. Rolling meadows, verdant pastures, leafy copses, babbling brooks, people's backsides pumping up and down on top of hayricks, village idiots being tormented by packs of crazed bloodhounds, any female still unwed by their fourteenth summer being ducked and then burnt as a witch, children being eaten alive by giant craneflies, raddled crones leaning on five-bar gates speculating about the size of the new parson's penis, and the steady thud of twelve-bore cartridges exploding in expensive Purdy box-lock ejector shotguns as simple country types moved through the landscape blasting away at anything with a face.

Cyril didn't much care for the countryside. You never knew what you were going to step into.

An old man came over. Turned-down wellies, tattered green corduroys held up with frayed orange baler twine and a grandad shirt spattered with cow shit. He clapped his hand on Cyril's shoulder, sighed, then pointed at the view.

'When I were a nipper, Michael, this was all fields and look at it now. Still, that's progress for you, I suppose,' he said sadly.

'It still is all fields, you daft old cunt, and the name's Cyril.'

'Shit, sorry, mate, wrong pub.'

When the tenth wasp aborted its kamikaze mission on Cyril's pint and decided to find out what was up Dawn's skirt, they went inside. Cyril paid the quid deposit required to get two splintered cues out from behind the bar, put ten pence in the pool table and racked 'em up.

A man came in, ordered a G & T and sat down to watch. Dawn let Cyril beat her four times. The man started giving Dawn all manner of helpful hints on how to improve her game. Cyril won twice more. The man wandered back to the bar, got a further G & T and returned holding a long black case stamped with gold initials. The cunt had his own cue.

Cyril v. the Cunt round one, was over in thirty seconds. Round two Cyril potted one ball and managed to spin the game out to nearly two minutes. Games three, four and five were the same, and at a tenner a time things were looking pretty good from where the Cunt was standing.

Cyril sank down heavily onto a red velvet stool. His hands quivered, his knees shook and his bottom lip began to tremble. The tears came. He flashed the Cunt a poor-boy look.

'Shit or Bust if you play the lady.'

The Cunt's jaw dropped. Pound signs flickered in his eyes. This really was his lucky day.

Cyril fiddled with the jumble of loose wires under the dash and the multiple-personality Rover spluttered back to life. He gunned the engine up to speed and selected a gear at random. The car lurched forward. As they chugged across the car park and back into the lane, Dawn counted a hundred quid in tenners into her handbag.

Three o'clock. The landscape started to change. The people were sweaty and stunted, the air smelled of cheap deodorant.

Cyril pulled the Rover on to a pub forecourt. The Wad and Mobile. Happy Hour. Outside, a bunch of lads wearing pink shell suits, no socks and white shoes. Lounging around a collection of Escorts and Sierras sporting full body kits, all possible bolt-on extras, fancy chrome wheels and monster sound systems, they were slamming each other's heads in their car doors, showing off in front of a gang of bottle-blonde lasses wearing identical white miniskirts, yellow Sir Cliff Richard on Tour T-shirts and black plastic high-heeled boots. The girls sported huge teeth, pumped-up tits and tiny raisin eyes set in puffed-up myxy rabbit faces. When they spoke, which was with great difficulty, they said 'sooper, luv-lee' or 'mod-elle', their voices like gusts of stagnant air seeping from the rectum of a dead horse.

So this was Essex.

Cyril and Dawn went in. They ordered a pint and a cocktail. It came to £19.97. Cyril found the pool table, paid the £50 deposit required to get two splintered cues out from behind the bar and put a two-pound coin in the slot. He racked 'em up and let Dawn serve.

A man came in. He crept up behind Cyril, got him in a death grip with one hand and emptied a pint of lager over Cyril's head with the other, then sharply introduced his knee into Cyril's bollock region.

Instinctively, Cyril knew exactly what to do. He spun round on his chubby heel, threw back his fat head, stretched out his porky arms and threw them around Television Ray.

'How are you my son? Don't you look smart. Lost a good few pounds I reckon, almost didn't recognise you there for a mo – and how come you're so bleedin' early? I thought I'd come down here, have a few sly ones and we'd meet up later. Anyway no bother, it's good to see you. So where's the little lady, the one I've been hearing so much about?'

Cyril got his breath back and motioned towards the pool table. From where he was standing Ray copped a glimpse of more tit than he'd seen in a very long time.

'Jesus H boy, is that yours? Blimey, you have done well for yourself, am I impressed or what? Oh yes, I am. Come here girl and say hello to Uncle Ray.'

Dawn moved towards him. Ray took her hand and kissed it.

'Sorry about that little display darlin', terrible waste of lager and wotnot but it's a thing from way back.'

'No problem Ray. I feel like doing that to him most of the time.'

Ray grinned. 'Reckon you've got a good'un there my son. Anyway, are you ready for the party or what?'

Cyril and Dawn followed Ray out of the Wad and Mobile, got their stuff from the Rover and slid into Ray's Renault Espace.

The people carrier swung down a narrow lane and stopped outside a pair of fancy wrought-iron gates. Ray hit a switch on the dash. The gates eased open, then swung shut behind the car as it crunched along a gravel drive which led up to the house. Dawn and Cyril glanced at each other, then at Ray.

'Clarsy eh?' Ray grinned.

The house was typical of the vernacular common to East Bergholt and the surrounding area. Constable country – Ray's neck of the woods. From the front it was a typical conversion, a row of thatched cottages knocked into one, tiny leaded mullioned windows and roses round the door.

'Watch this.'

Ray selected a pebble from the drive and lobbed it at the thatch. The pebble struck the apex, then bounced down the roof to the eaves, each bounce accompanied by a loud hollow thump.

'Fibreglass – lasts for ever and won't catch fire. Whatever will the bleedin' boffins think of next? Anyway, come in, come in. I'll show you to your room so you can freshen up. If you join me by the pool I'll introduce you to the missus.'

The interior of Ray's humble abode was cockney baroque. Fake Jacobean furniture, 100 per cent polyester medieval tapestries, black wrought-iron light fittings with plastic electric candles and overstuffed leather furniture. It made the Vatican look like a minimalist Japanese feng shui understatement. Dawn was gobsmacked and when Ray showed them to their room she nearly fainted with excitement. Gilded four-poster bed, pink satin sheets, lace-trimmed pillows, matching gold ormolu bedside tables with green onyx tops and a red fluffy shag pile a foot deep.

The en suite was even nicer. Black marble-effect wallpaper, Hollywood-style vanity mirrors, gold fittings throughout, a toilet that played the theme from *Mission Impossible* when you shat in it, a bidet that played 'Greensleeves' when you sat on it, a four-poster bath, and best of all a full suit of armour in the corner. Dawn was in heaven. Ray smiled at Cyril as she stretched out her hand to touch it.

'Just a sec my darlin'. Before you touch, please tell Uncle Raymond what you think it's made of?'

Dawn grinned. 'Bleedin' fibre-bleedin'-glass Ray, innit? Betcha it lasts for bleedin' ever and won't bleedin' catch fire.'

'Yep. How very bleedin' comical. You like it girl, you can have it, I've got a lock-up full of the bleedin' things.'

'As for you, Cyril my old mate, if you spot anything you fancy which'll fit in your horrible little motor, just say the word.'

'Aw cheers Ray, I'll take the bed.'

'Except the bed.'

'All right then, the bedside table thingies.'

'Blimey you cheeky cunt, they were mi muvver's. But anything else . . .'

'OK then. The fucking curtains.'

'Cyril didn't mean the curtains Ray.'

'Er, no, I didn't mean the curtains, Ray. All right, I'll think about it. Thanks.'

Cyril shaved, showered, shat in the professionally installed en suite which didn't leak at all, while Dawn fixed her make-up. They made their way downstairs and got lost. The house was bigger than it looked from the front. Out of sight of the prying eyes of planning authorities, Ray had extended the house back by a third of an acre. The rooms were massive and there were lots of them.

Half an hour later Dawn and Cyril found themselves in a tunnel. It was tiled, floor, walls and ceiling, and led them out into the garden. It smelt of sick.

'What you dozy fuckers doing using the peasants' entrance? Come over here and have a gargle.'

Ray was standing by the pool wearing his black silk dressing gown with red Chinese characters on the back. To the left of him a creature stretched out on a sunlounger.

'So did you like the extension or what? Big, innit? Thought I seen the ex-wife in there the other day, you know, clanking her chains wailing and wotnot. Anyway, this here is wife number two, her name's Sinf, short for Sinfi-ah. She's from near here, Chelmsford. Essex girl born and bred. This here's Cyril, Sinf, you know, the Yank – er no, that's some other geezer – and this here's Dawn, the new wife. Say hello to the nice people, darlin'.'

Cynthia stood up. She was wearing a tiny white bikini. Her hair was bright blonde, her skin tandoori red.

'Sooper luvlee mod-elle,' she croaked and the excitement was too much for her. A wet patch appeared on her bikini front bottom and it went see-thru. Cyril copped an eyeful of Cynthia's pubes. She wasn't a real blonde.

'For god's sake girl, go indoors and cover yourself up, we don't want to sit here staring at your soggy minge all bleedin' night do we girls and boys? No, I think we do not.

'Anyways, help yourselves to drinkies. The stuff's all stacked up in the pool but I'll get you the first ones in. Ladies' gear at this end, lager in the deep end.'

Ray stepped into the deep end. He went in up to his

ankles and walked right across. Six foot deep and five foot nine of it was cans.

Way off in the distance at the front of the house a car horn blurted the opening bars of 'Colonel Bogey'.

'Here we go, here we bleedin' go, here come the peasants, an' as you very well know girls and boys, the peasants are revoltin'.'

The maid ushered a bunch of young men wearing pink shell suits, no socks and white shoes out of the tunnel. They staggered on to the lawn. Their necks and faces bore the imprints of the edges of car doors. The young men took it in turns to try to pinch the maid's arse but they all failed dismally. They were already very pissed. One by one they fell. Some of the more determined carried on across the lawn on all fours before conking out, and two of the stronger ones stood up and careered hopelessly into the bushes.

There was another blast of 'Colonel Bogey' and a second group hit the lawn. The maid was far too nippy for them and they fell. The noise out front turned into the trumpet voluntary as car after car pulled up, parped its horn and disgorged wave after wave of the flower of Essex youth, who then bravely attempted to make it across the lawn. They stood shoulder to shoulder, their pink shell suits rubbing up against each other, the static making their hair stand on end and all the fibres fluff out of the cheap shiny fabric.

Ray turned to Cyril. 'Do you have any idea what it is like in the front garden at present my son? It is full of idiots. Chocka. That is why we have plastic plants.'

By now the lawn was littered with the prone fluffy pink bodies of the pissed-up, charged-up idiotic Essex undead and still they came. They knew no fear. Some of them got within striking distance of the pool but fell over anyway and the air was filled with their sickening cries.

Dawn heard a fanfare rising above the hubbub. It was the opening bars to Beethoven's Fifth. Four men in grey leisure suits emerged from the tile tunnel and confidently headed straight across the greensward. Stepping over failed pink bodies, the men in grey walked into the pool, reached below the surface and simultaneously cracked open matching cans of lager.

'Here we go, kids – it's the usual fuckin' suspects.'

'Nice to see you boys, 'specially coz you're the only cunts I invited in the first fuckin' place. Her indoors 'as gone indoors. We had a bit of a dingdong. I'm sorry to have to tell you she pissed her pants again, soppy kid.'

Right on cue Cynthia staggered out of the house, crying, pissing herself and brandishing a Bacardi Breezer like it was a watersports trophy. She straddled the first boy she came to, rubbed her tits on his chest and dripped Valium-tinged urine on to his face. He ran. Next one got the bazooka wee-wee treatment and did the same. Number three refused to budge till Cynthia began screaming in his ear. She shouted something about Alfie Tan and his horrible anus. The poor little sod dragged himself upright, shot through the tile tunnel and released himself back into the wild. Two minutes later the lawn was clear.

Cynth charged back into the house. Ray, Dawn, Cyril

and the boys watched as her crazed silhouette ran from room to room. She began screaming, clawing at her face and flashing the lights off and on, off, a pause, then on and off again – Morse code for PLEASE HELP ME I AM COMPLETELY MAD.

Transmission ceased. Cynth maintained radio silence and the house went dark.

'Anyway, the intro-bleedin'-ductions. This, boys, is Cyril. This boy just got wed and he was in such a bleedin' hurry he didn't think or have the time to think to invite yours truly to the wedding, so this is the point of tonight's little shindig soiree and wotnot. This other one here is Dawn. We've bin hanging out this avvy like the young 'uns say an' I think she's a diamond and clarsy with it. Anyway this little do is meant to be The Reception 2 – just when you thought it was safe to drink the bleedin' water – as I hear it was a bit pants when they had it up North. I'll introduce you to the boys an' we can get pissed in a mo. But first off I need to say somfink.

'Cyril, if you screw this one up I'll rip your bleedin' arms off an' shove 'em up yer arse. Dawn likewise. Godbless.

'A toast. Good elf. The 'appy couple. Be lucky.'

The men in grey fell into line. Ray threw his arms round Dawn and Cyril and led them along it. One by one he introduced them to the boys, each shaking hands like they were visiting royalty.

The drinking started. By ten the boys were up to their armpits in the deep end, the party atmosphere only slightly marred by Cynthia's brooding silhouette staring down from an upstairs window.

Cyril never left Dawn's side for a moment. He wanted to kiss her and she wanted to kiss him but each time they tried, the boys put their fingers in their gobs and made squelching noises with their armpits, which somehow broke the spell. Eventually, they slipped away behind the pool house and found a narrow path through the bushes leading to a clearing and a tiny hut. Cyril leaned up against it, grabbed Dawn and she folded into him all ready for a really serious gumsuck. The shed door creaked open and Ray stepped out. He invited them in. A candle guttering in a jam jar, a camping stool and a half-empty bottle of Teacher's.

'So you've found my little hidey-hole then, kids, where I comes if it all gets a bit much, when I need a breather, so to speak.'

He sank on to the canvas stool and cradled his head in his hands. Cyril slipped his arm round Ray's shoulder.

'Breather from what Ray?'

'From Sinf. I always do it, always have, always will, never bleedin' learn, always bleedin' do it.'

'Do what?'

'Feel sorry for 'em, take 'em 'ome, think maybe this time we can sort something out, but Jesus H, Cyril, you've seen Sinf and she's a bleedin' nutjob. When we first hitched up she was livin' in this 'orrible little gaff in Chelmsford selling windows days, doing barwork nights. I wanted to help her see, give her somethin' better, but when she moved in she turned. Went loopy and stayed that way. Thinks it's her territory now or something – even chases the bleedin' ducks.'

Dawn handed him the Teacher's.

'What will you do?'

'What can I do darlin'? Put up with it I s'pose, get up sparrowfart, work late and hide in me shed. What else is there? Sometimes I just feel like packing me bag and doing a bleedin' runner.'

'Well you can always come to us if you need a break, can't he, Cyril?'

Cyril nodded. 'Yeah, course.'

'Cheers kids, I might very well take you up on that one of these not so fine days. Anyway, time for the pressies I think.'

They staggered back along the path, met up with the boys, then trudged across the lawn, down the side of the house and out into the front garden. A huge silver-grey Mercedes crouched on the gravel drive. Alongside it the Rover, harnessed to the poshest caravan Cyril'd ever seen in his life. He was already working out how much he could get for it.

'Jesus H, Ray, you shouldn't have.'

'Narr narr, narr narr, narr. The van's just so you can carry the presents home. I 'spect you'll probably want to flog it anyway. The pressies are inside. And they're all bleedin' paid for. There's some classy gear in there, my son, far too bleedin' good for the likes of you but I 'spect Dawn will appreciate the stuff.

'We've had the Rover serviced this avvy, more like totally bleedin' rebuilt, so the garrige geezer tells me, so you should have no bother gettin' the stuff or the wife back home again.'

'Cheers Ray, I don't know what to say.'

The men in grey said goodnight. They scrambled into the Merc and roared off into the darkness.

'They're driving?'

'Yeah, Cyril, no bother with the old Bill round 'ere – Constable bleedin' country or not. Time for boo-boos I think.'

Dawn didn't get much sleep, she was far too excited. She wanted to open her presents and Cyril's snoring didn't help. When she finally did drop off she woke with a start twenty minutes later. She had a strange feeling. Tingling, like pins and needles only much more spiteful. Dawn felt it in her fingers, she felt it in her toes – just like in her favourite song written by the Troggs, nicely covered by REM, then murdered by Wet Wet Wet. She got dressed and went outside.

Dawn sat on artificial grass surrounded by plastic flowers and watched the sun come up. She'd never been so happy. She heard a rustle, and Ray sat down beside her.

'Mornin', princess. Sleep OK?'

'Not really. To be honest, I feel like shit.'

'What, bit of a hangover?'

'No, pains, really bad pins and needles.'

'Word of advice from Uncle Raymond, you want to get that checked out soon as poss, darlin'. Promise me you'll see the doc soon as you get 'ome. Mate of me mum's had simlar and it turned out – well, it weren't too clever anyway.'

Cyril woke at ten. He spent twenty minutes in the en suite – mostly with his head in the toilet, which also played the theme from *Mission Impossible* when you puked into it – went downstairs and joined his wife and Ray for breakfast.

Cyril fumbled for the jumble of loose wires under the dash. All gone. He twisted his key in the ignition, which was a new one on him, and nothing happened. He tried again and there was a shriek as the starter motor engaged with an engine which was already running. He wound down the window and the handle didn't fall off either.

'Fuckin' hell Ray, what've they done to this car?'

Ray clapped Cyril on the back, then leaned across him and handed Dawn a brown A4 envelope.

'For you princess. Don't open it till you get home.'

The Rover purred up the driveway, through the gates and out into the lane. Dawn and Cyril waved goodbye. Even dragging a caravan, the car went like shit off a shovel. They hit the North.

Soon as they got home Cyril dropped the jockey wheel, unhitched the caravan, wound down the jacks, found a new key on his keyring which fitted the 'van door and left Dawn to it.

Cyril sat alone in the Shakey. He sipped his Britvic and

smiled, imagining Dawn's face as she opened the presents.

By the time he reached Dawn's old flat it was dark and the street was empty. Cyril walked carefully along the pavement and stopped when he felt it wobble beneath his feet. He walked fifty paces back and waited. A woman came out of a sticky-stoned house three doors down and began loading boxes into a white Fiesta. In the orange sodium fizz of the streetlamp Cyril could see that she was a brunette, about thirty, five-six, nice tits but her arse was just a bit too big.

Cyril completely lost his bottle, but as he pictured Dawn's face when he had to tell her all the presents needed to be flogged to pay off his debts, Cyril found his bottle again. He set off briskly towards the woman.

Cyril hit the loose slab exactly square on. He felt a sharp pain in his leg and then, as his face smashed into the lamppost, which was an unexpected bonus, he blacked out.

Dawn unloaded the caravan, piled the presents in the front room, poured herself a nice big Malibu and set to work. First up was a big chunk of turned mahogany, which was a bit boring. Second up was another one, and as she dragged the wrapping off number three, Dawn realised what she'd got. A suppository four-poster. Dawn located the rest of the kit, which included detailed instructions (in German) and a small but perfectly inadequate toolkit, then lugged it all upstairs. Three hours later she'd put it up herself. She set about the rest.

Drapes, tapestries, brasses, beams, ormolu, onyx, plaster and flock. Everything she'd admired about Ray's gaff, present and correct.

Cyril peered through a slit in his bandages and noticed *The Hay Wain* bolted round the place at random. The stretcher bearers picked their way through a bedroom crowded with far too much oversized brand-new baroque furniture and carefully transferred Cyril on to pink satin sheets. They got him nice and comfy with lace-trimmed pillows and set his medication down on one of a matching pair of gold ormolu bedside tables with green onyx tops.

Dawn fetched him a whisky, and as he cradled the heavy cut-glass tumbler in his one good hand, watching topless women ice cubes drowning in thick amber fluid, Cyril came to terms with what he'd done. Broken ankle, broken wrist, splintered femur, fractured skull, broken nose, concussion, long-term psychological damage, resultant loss of earnings, panic attacks, paranoia, low self-esteem, stress, depression, significantly reduced quality of life and a witness. Perfect.

Next morning Dawn checked Cyril was still breathing. He was. She let him sleep. Dawn phoned Television Ray and told him all about the accident.

'Give that boy a bleedin' banana – not nearly as daft as he looks your old fella is he? Please pass on my sincere condolences and tell him nice goin' from me. I'll put yer on to a brief – name of Godfrey, posh git but sharp as a dart. No, best I talk to him first and he'll be in touch. Anyway, 'ave you opened your presents yet?'

'Yeah, they're great.'

'Smashin', glad you likes 'em. 'Spect the bed's already come in handy. You tell laughing boy try not to bleed on it – that's clarsy gear you got there, darlin'. And the envelope?'

'Shit no, I completely forgot.'

'You open that envelope, I'll get on to Godfrey, and we'll talk soon. Cheers for now.'

Dawn set the receiver down in its gold-plated cradle, went through to the kitchen to get the brown A4 envelope out her handbag.

There was a thunderous hammering at the front door. Dawn stepped into the hallway and saw a dark hulking figure silhouetted through the frosted glass panel. She thought about it for a moment, then opened the door six inches, jamming her foot against the bottom corner just in case.

The man was nearly seven feet tall, very thin, with huge watery eyes sunk deep into a palsied ashen face thatched with a mop of coarse white hair. He wore a long black raincoat, tight black shirt, anorexic black bootlace tie, black trousers, black socks and shiny black brothel creepers. He looked like one of the undead and his flies were undone.

Dawn shoved hard against the door but it was too late; his hairy paw shot through the narrow gap, seized her hand and grasped it tightly. Dawn screamed, then bit his hand.

'Allow me to introduce myself madam,' he boomed, 'Godfrey Napthene QC at your disposal maarm, and I'm so sorry but I always have this effect on people.'

'You're Ray's pal?'

'Yes indeed my good lady, the very same.'

'Well I'm sorry too, but bloody hell, that was quick. I was only on the phone to Ray two minutes ago.'

'I happened to be in the area madam. A comrade of mine from the Guards, you know – I was paying my respects to his dear widow. Raymond got me on the moby, I jumped in the motor and here I am.'

Dawn leaned past him. Out in the road a gleaming black Bentley dwarfed Cyril's Rover.

'Blimey, is that your car? You don't want to leave that parked round here.'

'Let me assure you madam. It is not a problem. Please do not trouble yourself on my account. If anyone so much as lays one finger on that car I shall instruct my associates to hunt them down and then I shall personally sue their bollocks off. Now are you going to let me in or what?'

She let him in. Godfrey lurched through to the kitchen. Dawn stuck the kettle on and fixed him a black coffee. He produced a slim black enamel cigarette case from the inside pocket of his long black mac, extracted a black Sobranie, sparked it up with a black lighter and frowned as Dawn shoved a green onyx ashtray across the table towards him.

'Hold on a sec Godfrey, I'm sure there's a black one

somewhere – in the front room I think. I'll fetch it you.'

'Thank you maarm, how kind of you to notice, and by the way this coffee tastes like shit. Nevertheless, I believe that despite your inability to prepare a half-decent brew and our rather shaky start we are now about to embark on a long and profitable friendship, if the information Raymond has imparted to me of your temperament and Cyril's condition are anything to go by.

'There's really no need to call me Godfrey, by the way. Godfrey is far too formal. You, my dear, may call me God.'

Cyril woke from an XXX-rated dream and noticed the grim reaper towering up at the far end of the four-poster with his flies undone. He screamed, wet himself and began to cry, begging for his life to be spared. Dawn drifted into view.

'Don't worry baby, I was scared too at first.' She smiled, stroking his head.

'This is God. He's here to help you.'

Godfrey familiarised Cyril with the underlying premise of the council's duty of care, their undeniable breach of that duty and their responsibilities therein in relation to the principles of the law of tort as outlined by Lord Justice Diplock in the notable case of Lister vs. Romford Ice and Cold Storage Co. Ltd 1966 and consolidated by Lord Justice Greer regarding Doyle vs. Olby (Ironmongers) 1969. Cyril lay there shivering in a lake of his own piss, listening as God droned on and on. It dawned on him that he'd made a terrible mistake and he lost the will to live. He began to cry again.

'So there you have it,' Godfrey bellowed, 'that's the legal side covered – all a bit tiresome I'm afraid but:

(A) I feel that you should be in possession of the basic facts and
(B) aware of exactly what my 25 per cent entails but
(C) you can rest assured that when the council's tinpot legal department see my moniker on the notepaper they'll
(D) shit themselves and
(E) the case will never go to court.
(F) I intend to procure a substantial interim payment and then
(G) argue about the rest. So
(H) you, my good man, are going to be rich.'

Dawn smiled. Godfrey smiled back. Cyril wet himself again.

The photographer showed up. Roger Smarm took a quick bedshot to establish the incontinence, then he and Dawn hoisted Cyril into an ice-cold bath so the bruising showed up really nicely. Dawn stripped the bed. Roger got busy. Cyril looked bad before but now, what with the water, a little judiciously applied marker pen and the additional injuries caused by the laughter, Cyril's full-length star and victim centrefold pics for *Nasty*

Accident Monthly looked like Barry McGuigan mangled by a monster truck and back from the dead.

Stifling a yawn with the back of her hand, Dawn felt her stomach heave as she leafed through a four-year-old copy of *The People's Friend*. Bored by the cheesy romances, the recipes, the crap knitting patterns and worried shitless, she waited her turn for Assee the black doctor. Her left eye slipped out of focus and she laid the magazine back on the table with all the others.

The bell rang. Eileen on reception called out her name and Dawn picked her way down the scruffy pastel corridor that led to Assee's office. She sat down and told him what was up. Assee said 'Try not to worry' and booked her in for tests. Five minutes later Dawn was out in the road, her head full of questions she'd either forgotten or was too scared to ask.

Her left eye went fuzzy again and this time the right followed suit. Dawn sat heavily on a garden wall studded with stale grey chuddy and fresh white bird shit. Her hands and feet crackled with pain. She felt it every hour on the hour almost every day. The tingling was getting worse.

The phone rang as Dawn unlocked the front door. It was Assee. 'Not always true what they say about the health service, is it?' he said. 'Your tests are tomorrow morning.'

Dawn went upstairs, found Cyril propped up in bed surrounded by brochures, bottle of Teacher's on the go. She lay down on the bed beside him. Cyril kissed her and ran his bandaged fingers through her hair. She decided not to tell him.

> There's no doubt about it, a mobility vehicle can make a tremendous difference to your life!!! From being stuck in the house dependent upon family and friends for trips out, suddenly you are able to make your own decisions once again about WHERE and WHEN you are going!

'The pub. Now,' Cyril muttered, draining his fifth whisky.

> These days you're almost bound to see a scooter or powerchair user when you are out in town, down at the local shops or on a day out! They are very popular machines and with good reason – just chat to one of the owners and they'll tell you how they could never imagine being without their 'new pair of legs!'

'Anyway are there different models to choose from?' Cyril mouthed the words from the guidebook and drained his sixth whisky.

> Yes, quite a few! Let's take the scooters to start with!!!

Cyril flicked through the bumf and stopped at the first picture he came to. A white-haired old bird sitting proudly astride a red Sundancer three-wheel power-chair scooter which provided her with the ultimate scooter-riding experience as she cruised the aisles of her local garden centre.

Stylish, rugged and dependable, her new Sundancer exuded unmatched scooter power and versatility. Comfort and style came as standard. Freedom and flexibility never looked so good.

Cyril turned the page. A limited-edition range from Rascal Electric Mobility. The same old lady at the tiller of a blue Celebrity XL offering all the performance, stability, safety and comfort you could shake a walking stick at, stunning good looks that encompassed the most modern design techniques in flowing curves, metallic paint and stylish alloy wheels.

The Celebrity XL benefited from a top speed of eight mph, a travelling radius of twenty miles, and featured a handy wire basket mounted on the prow containing a rolled-up newspaper, Dick Francis's latest novel, a bottle of Spa mineral water, two green peppers, an apple and a lemon. It looked plenty big enough for six cans of lager and a take-away chinky.

The old girl was parked up by a mossy five-bar gate, chatting to a smiling young blonde wearing mauve open-toe sandals, tight light-blue pedal pushers and a skimpy strapless cerise top. Cyril couldn't quite make out the blonde's arse from the angle the photo was taken at, but she was about five six, with good legs, medium-sized tits and a vacuous obliging face.

Cyril's eyes perved holes in the picture. He liked what he saw.

Cyril powered his brand-new metallic-blue limited-edition Celebrity XL down the hill, bucking and choking in the oily slipstream of a sixteen-wheeler DAF Tautliner diesel. Up ahead, a traffic sign which had never bothered him before: inside a red-framed triangle a tiny silhouetted car descended a steep black wedge with 4% reversed out in white. Cyril felt his guts drop. Four per cent chance of survival. They'd never mentioned that in the bumf.

When he reached the main road Cyril took his life in his hands and hung a right. The Celebrity XL burrowed through a snarling column of oncoming traffic, made it into the relative safety of the car park and crawled in through the automatic doors of recently refurbished Netto.

As the doors slid shut behind him, Cyril pulled up, rearranged his bowels and eased his body forwards. He fished the list which Dawn had left him from his handy front-mounted basket. His right elbow snagged the direction lever and the XL shot straight into a pile of wire baskets. The impact jolted Cyril backwards and his elbow set the XL into reverse. The top twenty of the heap of carriers came down on top of him and Cyril threw himself forwards, trying to hide his head under the microscopic dashboard. His elbow caught the lever again and the XL lurched forwards. This time the whole lot came down. Cyril's 'new pair of legs' were crippled already, stymied at the centre of an hilarious metal puzzle, hours of fun for all the family but not really suitable for children under twelve, trapped in a jumbled wire cage festooned with onion husks, forgotten discount vouchers and discarded shopping lists. He called out for help but for a full five minutes nothing came, except shame and inferiority, which came as standard.

Two smirking lads emerged from behind a shrink-wrapped pallet of dog food. Their dull skin pitted with acne, their hair filthy, and their blotched greasy faces wearing the same puzzled look, like they'd been caught wanking.

They pulled the carriers off, grunting and sweating as they worked towards the centre of the heap, giving Cyril the full benefit of their stinking pits as they took it in turns to lean across him. Cyril thanked God Dawn wasn't here to see this.

The dirty boys yanked off the last two carriers and tossed them to one side, freeing the gleaming hull of the Celebrity XL. A smattering of impolite applause washed over the small crowd which had gathered to watch and a photographer from the local paper stepped forward to record the moment for a crap local news item about local people living in Cyril's local area. Cyril spun the mean machine through 180 degrees and faced his local public. Utilising the handy front-mounted basket as a kamikaze sighting device, he aimed the XL at the densest part of the throng and jammed the direction lever forwards.

Unmatched scooter power and versatility, stunning good looks that encompassed the most modern design techniques in flowing curves, metallic paint and stylish alloy wheels, could easily put several very unhelpful local people in their local outpatients when used as a weapon. Eight miles an hour felt pretty quick indoors.

Out in the car park Cyril decided exactly where and when he wanted to go and ten minutes later the rumble of tyres on tarmac was replaced by the swish of tyres on dodgy patterned carpet and another round of applause as he slipped into the comfy twilight of the Shakespeare Hotel.

The telly at the far end of the bar, permanently tuned to local TV, flickered fuzzy black-and-white security footage of a crazed and as yet unidentified local power-chair user callously ramraiding a terrified knot of concerned local onlookers in a local supermarket only minutes ago, local time.

Safe inside his local Cyril trundled the XL towards a vacant table, didn't bother to pull up a seat coz he'd brought his own, and waited while Dave the landlord fetched a pint over 'on the house', which was the first time in the entire history of the Shakespeare Hotel est. 1840 and run by three generations of the same cantankerous, penny-pinching family, that either of these things had ever happened.

Cyril glugged a big mouthful of free pint number one and relaxed. He pictured Dave as a smiling young blonde wearing mauve open-toe sandals, tight light-blue pedal pushers and a skimpy strapless cerise top. Cyril couldn't quite make out his arse from the angle the Celebrity XL was parked at, but Dave was about five six, with good legs, medium-sized tits and a vacuous obliging face. Cyril felt an hour's worth of adrenalin drain from his shattered body and squidged his aching backside deep into the luxuriously padded, generously posture-sprung seat of his trusty limited-edition Celebrity XL. Cyril necked his pint and almost immediately Dave fetched him another. Everything was cool. Comfort and stability came as standard. Freedom and flexibility never felt so good.

Dawn lay on her side facing the dog-eared Charlie Brown poster which was supposed to take her mind off everything. Sister rattled in with her trolley, ordered her to bring her knees tight under her chin and wait for Doctor Tarquin who was a very busy man.

Dawn glanced over at the trolley, scuffed grey rubber wheels, chipped cream frame, empty middle shelf, top shelf lined with crispy white tissue. Eighteen-inch stainless-steel sigmoidoscope, industrial-size blue and white tube of KY, speculum like one of the profile contraptions she used to keep hers and Cyril's absolute favourite boots in shape, a chrome-framed rubber-headed mallet and a metal-bound syringe big enough to ice a wedding cake.

Doctor came in with his clipboard. Cleared his throat, smoothed his tie, flicked back Dawn's white hospital gown, raised an eyebrow at the rose tattoo on her buttock and patted her bum rather more than necessary. 'Slight amount of discomfort.' He opened her rectum with his thumb and index finger, then inserted the sigmoidoscope up to the hilt. Dawn gasped, felt her insides shrivel and the blood slow in her veins. Doctor operated a trigger mechanism and somewhere deep inside Dawn's bowels a claw snipped away a piece of flesh from her lower intestine and withdrew it for tests.

'On your back, feet together, knees apart.'

Dawn did as she was told and stared up at a tattered gorilla/kitten poster taped to the ceiling. He inserted the speculum and had a good long look at her cervix.

'On your front now.'

The needle. A blunt bruising blow to the spine, a wasp diving in armed with house brick and dagger, puncture, steel jostling between vertebrae, then a terrible feeling like the juice being sucked. 'Fine, sit up now please.' He tip-tapped her knees with the mallet. Tarquin made notes and flounced out. Dawn went back to her cubicle and dressed.

She phoned a taxi from reception. 'Yeah, OK, ten minutes. Staff car park just off B-road.' Dawn drifted out through the main doors, found the place and sunk down on the low newly repointed perimeter wall. Five feet away a metallic red BM with a personal plate and the sunroof open. A manicured hand dangling a Rothman's king-size from the driver's window, platinum watch, soft pink wrist, expensive shirt. Relaxed, self-satisfied conversation, educated laughter. Doctor Tarquin and his brother.

'Quite frankly Quentin, I'd rather fuck a dead plastic pig with yours old boy, than stick my highly qualified medical todger in that flaky little hole. You know it's malignant MS, don't you? Six weeks tops. Next time the earth moves for that one they'll be covering her up with it. Bet she likes it up the dirtbox, though, eh? Nice bum, rose tattoo, the horny little filly, good tight rectum too, nearly had my finger off – one for Miles the piles, I think. Specialist arse man, not sure if you've met him yet, stick anything up there for a laugh, strictly in the interests of science, dontcha know? He'd really make the cow's feet tingle, give the poor bitch a proper send-off, ha ha ha.'

The taxi came.

Dawn unlocked the front door and went inside. No Cyril. She phoned his mobile and reached him down the Shakey. *Couldn't get the shopping, been on telly, Dave's arse, freedom and flexibility, see you later babe.*

She went through to the kitchen, shoved the kettle on, lost her balance and fell. Dawn lay sobbing on the cold lino floor. She noticed all the shit down the side of the cooker: fragmented spud, desiccated peas, shrivelled carrots, withered onions, ancient rice and antique pasta – so that's how they invented Pot Noodle. Suddenly she could murder one. She lay on the floor laughing.

The kettle clicked off. Dawn dragged herself upright and smoothed down her dress. A metal fist in her gut, coarse grey static in her right eye, numbness rising up her legs and a ridiculous feeling of euphoria. No point in saying owt. Comes to us all soon enough. Christ.

Dawn went in her handbag for sweeteners and found the brown A4 envelope. Stuck for hours in a waiting room, nothing to see, nothing to read, fear brewing up inside her and all the while a surprise burning away in her bag.

She tore it open. A lavish glossy brochure. The most

breathtakingly beautiful creation she'd ever laid eyes on. Little stone people, horses, hats and castles, a green and white chequerboard shot thru with gold, and a wild frothing description of the difference a hand-crafted, special-edition, limited-availability, once-in-a-lifetime collector's-item chess set would make to her life. Close-ups of each piece, a potted life history of the Sicilian peasant responsible for its conception, carving and design, and a detailed schedule of delivery over the next six weeks.

Dawn reached for the phone and dialled Ray's number. One drring, then somebody picked up.

' 'Ello, Chelmsford windows and doors, Cynfia speaking and 'ow may I help yoooooooo?'

'Cynthia?'

'Yes and 'ow may I help yoooooooooo?'

'Ray's wife?'

'Yes and 'ow may I help yoooooo?'

'It's Dawn, is Ray there please?'

'Er, no 'fraid 'ees not 'ere at present.'

'When does he get back?'

'Er, dunno, 'ees not 'ere at present so's I can't ask 'im. Tell ya wot, I'll ask when 'ee gets back when will 'ee be back.'

'Great. Thanks, Cynth, I'll speak –'

'Is that Alfetanu talking?'

'What?'

'Is you Alfetanu?'

'Alfie who?'

'Naar naar, A L F E T A N U.'

'What?'

'Is you Alfetanu?'

'No dear, you must be mixing me up with someone else.'

''Oo?'

'Sorry?'

''Oo is I mixin' you up wiv?'

'I don't know Cynthia, I really don't know.'

'Is it me then?'

'What?'

'Is I Alfetanu?'

'No, I don't think so, love, you're Cynth, Ray's wife. Remember?'

'Oh yeah, sooper lov-lee.'

'Listen Cynth, you sound a bit confused, are you OK?'

'No, no I'm not, I'm not OK, I'm stuck 'ere on me tod an' I don't know 'ow to open the windas.'

'Well I'm sure Ray'll show you when he gets back.'

'Ray?'

'Jesus . . . Ray. Ray your husband. Television Ray. Anyway, great talking to you again. Bye.'

'What the fuck was that all about?' Dawn asked her brand-new mugtree, plucking World's Greatest Lover from its topmost branch. She sorted out an instant coffee, took it through to the front room, pushed aside nets, scrubbed away tears and stared out into the dark. No point in worrying. No sense in spoiling things. Not just yet. Comes to us all. Shit.

A light burning in the caravan, something moving about inside.

Dawn selected a black marble ashtray, crept out of the house, inched her way down the fractured tarmac driveway and eased back the door to the 'van. In the dining area neat piles of clothes ranged along the fluffy orange bench seating. An open suitcase on the tiny fold-down Formica table. Someone bent over unpacking it, humming quietly to themselves.

Dawn breathed in hard and raised the ashtray high above her head, clutching it with both hands like a polystyrene rock in the caveman films.

Her right eye blurred, the vertical hold went in the left and she brought the black marble lump down heavily and way off target, completely destroying a handy eye-level storage facility and splintering the majority of its compact melamine two-person dinner-service contents.

The intruder turned to face her. A pair of golf shoes in each hand, half a dozen silk ties thrown over his left shoulder.

'Evenin' princess.'

'Ray?'

Cyril eased cream cavalry-twill slacks down around his ankles, gingerly extracted his penis from purple nylon jockeys, then desperately tried to maintain conversation and avoid eye contact while Dave wedged a copper-coloured waste bin between his knees and waited for Cyril to do his business.

'Not strictly part of my job this pal, you'll be wanting a fucking bedbath next.'

'Sorry Dave.'

'Are you done?'

'Yeah, cheers mate. Sorry about that but when you gotta go you've . . .'

Cyril's mobile rang. Dawn again. *Come straight home, fetch some take-outs, got company, big surprise, darling, bye.*

'Gotta go. The wife. Eight bottles of Newky and a Malibu, please – I'll sort the cash tomorrow.'

Dave loaded the drinks into the Celebrity XL's handy front-mounted basket. Cyril hit the direction lever and zipped out into the car park. Christ, it felt cold. Someone shouting his name. Cyril spun the XL round. Dave's head sticking out the pub back door, tears streaming down his face.

'Dave? What's up pal? Please don't cry, I've really gotta go now, talk about it tomorrow, OK?'

Dave cracked him a massive grin, first one Cyril could ever remember.

'Pull yer trousers up, eh, Cyril? There's a good lad. Night.'

Dawn settled Ray in the front room, shut the curtains and stuck the fire on. He produced a silver hip flask and poured a couple of large ones. Ray told Dawn how he'd left home, left Cynth, couldn't cope any more with the Valium, the incredible crushing stupidity and worst of all the public incontinence. Naughty of him he knew, but the caravan had always been an option.

'Anyway how are you my darlin'?'

'Ray, I'm not sure if I should really . . .'

'Blimey, your milkman's a bit previous in't he? It's only eleven thirty.'

Outside the whirr of an electric motor and the clink of bottles, then a piteous cry as Cyril seriously misjudged the XL's turning circle and smashed directly into the offside rear of his own car.

Ray drew back a heavy velvet drape and twitched aside the net.

'Aha, the happy wanderer returns to the bosom of his family after an hard night's toil at the fluid-testing laboratory. But alas! just as all seems well, tragedy strikes and he tumbles from his pushchair. Oh dearie, dearie me. Your brave and handsome husband's belly up in the road my darlin'. Shall we fetch the poor boy indoors?'

Dawn swished back front-room curtains and winced as radioactive death-ray morning sunlight blasted twin holes in her skull. She cleared away last night's empties, opened the front door to get some air and perched on the step sucking it down like Alka-Seltzer.

Sitting at the table in his new compact home, M-People blasting out, a mobile wedged under his chin and a china teacup cradled in his right hand, Ray was busy on his laptop. She waved.

He made the international glass/can/bottle-to-mouth gesture and clutched his forehead. Dawn smiled and did the same. Out in the road a blue Transit pulled up alongside Cyril's dinted Rover and a man stepped out. He picked his way down the shattered path, stumbling over the new orange cable which fed power to the caravan, handed Dawn a clipboard and set a box at her feet. She signed for the package and went inside.

Dawn tore away corrugated cardboard wrapping. Three packages: a big flat one and two smaller parcels. She started with the largest, unpicked yards of stubborn brown parcel tape from truculent opaque bubble pack and set a green and white chequered mahogany-framed board on the kitchen table.

She set about number two. A leaflet fluttered out:

> Verde Antico This beautiful green marble is a brecciated serpentine characterised by various-sized patches of white, black and dark green, interspersed with a network of streaks in varying tones of green. It was being quarried at Thessaly in Greece more than 2,000 years ago; the source was then lost, and only rediscovered less than a century ago!

It was the pawns. Grinning under green wicker panniers, their stunted green limbs twisted by the weight of their heavy green burdens, they were supposed to be medieval woodcutters going about their simple rustic business, but as Dawn strung them out in a wonky green row across the board's second rank, they became a bunch of petrified children off on a picnic with far too much green stuff.

Dawn laid into the last package. Another leaflet:

> Sienna This well-known type of variegated white marble is named after the Italian province in which

> it is quarried. Throughout the ages it has been highly esteemed for its richness, warmth, variety of colouring and harmonious relationship with other marbles. It is not uncommon to find tints of pale cream, rosy red, grey and deep yellow, broken by veins of black purple, reddish grey and brown, all softly blended and forming a pleasing harmony of sequence with the predominant white ground!

More pawns. White medieval woodcutters, albino children convulsed by the weight of far too many white loaves, stumbling off to happiness – a white kids-only milk-based picnic on the white cliffs of Dover.

Dawn went outside and knocked the caravan door. Ray opened and she went inside.

'Stuff in the box all right for you darlin'?'

'Yeah, thanks Ray. The board and lots of little ones. They're great but I haven't the faintest how you play.'

'Don't you worry 'bout that girl. When we have the full S.P. I'll teach yer myself.'

'Cheers, Ray. I look forward to that. How long before it's all here?'

'Them little bleeders are the pawns. You want rooks, knights, bishops, kings and queens, so at one delivery per week, that makes another five weeks before we do the business.'

'Five weeks?'

The post lady parked her trolley, strolled up the path and handed Dawn two envelopes through the open caravan window. One for her and one for Cyril, which looked important. He was still asleep so she took an executive decision and opened them both.

Dawn's was an appointment with her GP to discuss test results, Cyril's a *with compliments* from Godfrey Napthene Associates and a cheque for £750,000. She shoved it across the table to Ray.

'Fuck me! 'Scuse me, darlin', but God is good in't he? And this is only the interim payment you know, there'll be plenty more where this little lot come from. Do you have Cyril's details?'

'What?'

'Account number, sort code etc.?'

'Yeah, why?'

'I thought we'd deposit the cheque and keep shtoom about it to laughing trousers till it's cleared. That way his joy will be instant and the poor boy will be able to get his grubby hands on the loot a.s.a.p. Check on him now darlin', tell him we're off out and we'll get it sorted.'

After they'd paid in the cheque, Dawn and Ray wandered through town.

Dawn window-shopped. For the first time in her life she could have anything she wanted and she didn't fancy any of it.

Clothes seemed frivolous, colours fading, designs dating and stitches bursting even as she looked at them. Shoes were even worse. The soles would wear, the leather crackle, they'd split and leak, then the heels would come off. Consumer durables held no appeal; doomed to the rust and disrepair lurking microns under their shiny white cellulose and matt black surround-sound, total home-cinema entertainment systems were unentertaining, unreliable dust traps. They'd never look as clean or sound half so nice as they did in the shop, and after a lifetime supply of crappy quiz shows, half-baked telethons, soulless music and bad news had dribbled through their fragile transistorised guts, their joints would dry, their PCBs malfunction and you'd have to thump them to get a picture, a song or just one last sickly dose of light ent.

They could keep the lot. It was a pile of useless, trivial, pointless, depressing, overpriced shit. All Dawn wanted was the rest of her chess set, Cyril, Ray and a drink.

Ray suggested the country. Ten minutes later they were in it, cruising through soft dark glades, climbing harsh rock-strewn hillsides and motoring across high bracken-clad moorland. Dawn had lived in the same dirty little town her whole life with no notion of this peaceful beauty on her doorstep and it was far too fucking late for that now.

The people carrier pulled off the road into the car park of the first decent-looking boozer they came to. The pub garden overlooked a reservoir. Victorian engineers with tall hats, large houses and even bigger ideas had built a huge parabolic stone dam complete with pointed medieval valve houses across a wooded river valley and watched it fill – the same water Dawn had bathed in, cooked with and used to flush the toilet all her life fifteen minutes down the road.

It was flat calm. Way out in the centre fish were priming in the late afternoon sun, taking mayflies off the surface film.

Ray brought the drinks over.

'Did you know the mayfly has no arse, my darlin'?'

'Eh?'

'They hatch, live for one day, shag, then snuffit. They don't eat so they don't, erm . . . need the khazi.'

'Really Ray, how absolutely fascinating.'

'And did you know for example, that there is no name for the back of the knee and that wasps cannot be sick?'

'Really? And fascinating fact number four is . . .?'

Ray leaned forward. 'Princess, do you know if you weren't already hitched, if things were different and perhaps if you felt similar.'

'Yeah, I did know that one Ray. Me too.'

She took his hand. Through the tears in her eyes she could see the tears in his eyes.

'Listen Ray, there's something I need to tell you –'

At the far end of the valley the distant honking of a hundred rubber and brass vintage-car hooters destroyed the moment. A big grey join-the-dots W in the sky came in lower and lower and as it got closer the skein of Canada geese reorganised themselves into V-formation, three birds at the front doing dosey-do, taking turns to play squadron leader. They dropped black-webbed landing gear and waterskied to a standstill, sending bow waves lapping up against both banks.

Dawn told him. She told Ray about the pain, the numbness, the intermittent blindness, the fear, the fall, the Pot Noodle and the timescale, how she'd overheard what was up with her, that her appointment was at four tomorrow but she was convinced already. She begged Ray not to tell Cyril and made him promise he'd take care of him. Dawn cried until the snot ran down her face. Ray held her and stroked her hair until the sobbing stopped. He proffered the softest silk hanky. Dawn emptied her nose into it and felt much better.

They called in at the Shakey on the way home, just on the off chance, the faint possibility, the completely dead cert that Cyril would be in there. He was. Parked at his favourite table by the mucky calendar. Snuggled up with a blonde girl, tight cerise top and a vacuous obliging face.

They joined him. He'd had to crawl down the stairs and it'd taken him a full fifteen minutes to straddle the XL before he'd realised his wallet was still upstairs on the bedside table, but Dave had tabbed it and could Ray possibly lend him a tenner? Ray rolled his eyes at Dawn and bunged Cyril a monkey.

By closing Dawn couldn't feel her legs at all and everything she saw was double. She didn't know if it was the booze or the illness or both but as she sat there with one arm around Ray and the other round Cyril, doing daggers at the blonde bitch, Dawn really didn't give a fuck. She was free.

> The first issue that confronts the doctor looking after a person with multiple sclerosis is when to discuss and name the diagnosis. Once the diagnosis is strongly suspected or confirmed, it is appropriate

> to break this news, which, given the increase in public awareness of medicine in general and MS in particular, rarely comes as a surprise to patients with tell-tale symptoms. However, there will be occasions when the diagnosis does come as a thunderbolt and for this reason we prefer to break the news in a few sentences which move from confirmation that the symptoms are significant, that they indicate an illness affecting the CNS, that they suggest a tendency for patches of inflammation (with suitable metaphors to explain this term) in the brain or spinal cord and that a high proportion of people in whom this pattern develops turn out to have an illness known as multiple sclerosis. Some remarks on self-help usually follow.
>
> Further questions may arise but this consultation can usually be completed in 30–35 minutes.

Assee snapped the heavy book shut and pushed it aside. He straightened his tie then pressed the white bell-push taped to the leg of his desk.

Footsteps in the corridor, then the door creaking open. Dawn came in. Assee motioned to the grubby plastic chair which faced him. She sat.

He told her that her recent tests confirmed the symptoms which she had already described, that they indicated an illness affecting the CNS, and that they suggested a tendency for patches of inflammation (he couldn't think of any suitable metaphors to explain this term) in the brain or spinal cord and that a high proportion of people in whom this pattern develops turn out to have an illness known as multiple sclerosis. Some remarks on self-help followed.

Dawn said thank you but she already knew and was it true about malignant MS? He said yes, any time now. The consultation was completed in ten minutes.

She went home. Her hand dead as she tried the front door, then her legs. The door swung open and she fell into the hallway. No sign of the XL; a set of keys on the mat. She picked herself up, stumbled through to the kitchen and put the kettle on. Dawn stirred two spoonfuls of instant into a mug of boiling water, flicked the spoon round clockwise and watched crunchy black grains dissolve into thin brown fluid.

She tried Cyril's mobile. Switched off. Please try later. She phoned the Shakey. Dave muffled the receiver, then said he'd not been in. She heard the lie in his voice and Cyril laughing in the background. She went down there. Early-doors pensioners huddled round the telly watching *Countdown*, light slanting low through bobbled glass panes illuminating pints and smoke. Heads on fire spewing thin blue clouds, glowing beers centre stage of an undiscovered ready-made late-afternoon drinks commercial. Dawn clocked Cyril. Saw him sat with Miss Tight Cerise Top. Her hand on his crotch, his tongue halfway down her throat.

Dawn flounced across sticky patterned carpet and slapped his face. Made a show of herself and spilled his bitter. The pensioners lost interest in *Countdown*.

Dawn drew back her fist, caught her reflection in the Murphy's mirror and felt pain fizzing in her elbow. She split his lip and left.

Dawn dropped the latch on the Yale just to be sure. She packed Cyril's clothes, his medication, lugged them downstairs, then packed the charger for the XL and the heads. She went back up to the bedroom and cast around for anything else. His wallet on the onyx bedside table. Sod that she thought and pocketed it. Somebody knocking at the front door. She flicked back the bedroom net. Ray standing outside clutching a plastic water carrier.

' 'Scuse me darlin', but I need a refill. Anyway, how are you and what's all this gear in aid of?'

She took his hand and led him through to the kitchen, fetched sherry from the front room. Dawn sat down opposite Ray at the kitchen table and poured two big ones.

'So where's laughing boy today then darlin' – out on is brand-new pushchair, I bet?'

'He's down the Shakey. Half an hour back I caught Cyril with that blonde lass, you know the one from last night.'

'What?'

'Yeah. Caught him snogging her in public. That's his stuff out in the passage. I've got his wallet and his keys and I don't ever want to see him again.'

'Well I do and let me tell you darlin', when I find that slimy –'

'Shut up, Ray. I'm not one of your fucking damsels in distress.'

Ray shrank back in his chair. 'Dawn, whatever's wrong, princess? 'Ave I done something to upset you?'

She bowed her head and addressed the chequerboard lino floor.

'It is malignant MS Ray. Assee says so. Not long to go now.'

'Shit. That's not clever. Mate of me mum's . . .'

'Ray, please, shut it. Let me say this.'

She looked up at him. His face grey and her eyes spilling over.

'When I die Ray, drive me back to that lake. Cook me up, then chuck me in. Put me in the soup with all the mayflies. Insects with no arse. Just hang around till then. Now for fuck's sake help me get the stuff shifted before I cry again.'

They worked in silence and without eye contact, each afraid that a word or look would tip the other over, propel them into uncontrollable rage and grief. Ray packed his things and left them in the drive. They moved Cyril's stuff into the caravan, then Ray's into the house.

They slumped down in the front room, stuck the telly on to break the silence and waited. Ray fished a bottle of Teacher's out his suitcase, made a medicine joke and they drank it, flinching each time a leaf, a can or a cat blew up the drive. They both expected Cyril to come back, they wanted him to, they wanted to tell him, to crush his spirit, then his balls, to use the truth as a weapon, to make him pay for what he'd done and blame him for what he hadn't, but he didn't.

The Teacher's ran out at three. They slept where they sat.

Next morning Ray woke first. Dragged himself off the sofa, drew back the curtains and rubbed his eyes. He focused on Dawn. Blood on her face and a brown patch between her legs. He ran a bath, shipped her upstairs and eased her fully clothed into clear, cold water. She was still unconscious.

Ray began stripping off her wet clothes. He pulled her sodden dress up over her head and chucked it in the basin, then took her shoulders, bent her forwards and unclipped her bra. Dawn came to, thought he was Cyril and put her arms around him. She went to kiss him, then realised, remembered and threw up all over Ray. He wiped himself down with toilet roll and flushed it away. She lay in the bath sobbing, adding her own salty contribution to the fresh cold fluid. Ray left her to soak. He went downstairs and cleared up.

Dawn towelled herself dry, put on clean clothes and went down. She felt fine. Ray at the kitchen sink scrubbing furiously at a beige velour cushion cover.

'How did you know to do that, the bath?'

'Ah, well, my darlin', while you was out yesterday at the doc's and then the Shakespeare I got on the blower, pals of mine in the medical line style of thing. Cold baths are supposed to be the business. You look loads better princess.'

'Yeah, I feel fine. What's with the spring-cleaning and that smell? Christ, it smells like someone's . . . oh shit no, I didn't did I? Oh, Ray, please tell me I didn't.'

'Yes my darlin', I'm afraid you did, um, how can I put it nice? Shit yourself, which is normal for a person with your affliction. You, my darlin', I'm sorry to have to say, would make a really rubbish mayfly.'

Dawn laughed until her nose bled. It happened again. An amoeba of warm brown slurry oozing across the kitchen floor. Ray on his hands and knees soaking it up with a teacloth, Dawn bent over the kitchen table shitting herself with laughter. Ray got up and rinsed the cloth out in the sink. He made himself look as stern as possible, then stared into her eyes, struggling to keep a straight face.

'Well princess, I'm very 'appy you find it all so bleedin' comical. So far this morning you've ad two nose bleeds, two little accidents and been sick all over Uncle Raymond's favourite shirt and it is still only nine thirty. You've been a very, very, very bad girl. This kitchen is my responsibility now, and nobody, I repeat nobody, shits in here without my say-so. Bathtime for you again young lady.'

Dawn went upstairs and ran another bath. Ray could hear her laughing as she splashed about. He cleaned the floor, then sat down at the kitchen table. He thought about her body, her arms around him and her soft breasts falling forward as he undid her bra. Ray shoved his fingers in his mouth and bit them to stem the sobbing. He dried his eyes and washed his face in the sink. He made coffee, pasted on a smile and took it up to her. She was still laughing.

Ray decided on a banquet. Convinced himself it was a good idea. A proper feast, posh nosh with all the trimmings. He went downtown for supplies: food, flowers, fruit, booze and sweets, Twiglets and chocolate. Ray bought himself a pricey silk shirt and an even more expensive dress for Dawn. A black crushed-velvet number, twin spaghetti straps, a crazy carefree hemline and a stark raving bonkers adults-only neckline.

As he swung the people carrier back up the hill, Ray saw the shiny stern of the XL sloping in through the side door of the Shakey. He jammed the anchors on and pulled over. Ray fished a socket wrench out the glove compartment, thought about it and decided not. It was beneath him.

Ray pushed open the front door and went through to the kitchen. He set all the shopping on the table, then fetched a vase from the china cabinet in the front room. He half filled it with cold water, extracted flowers from romantically patterned paper and slid them carefully from their crispy cellophane sheath. He released the thick blue elastic band which bound their stems then crushed the end of each stalk with his thumb so they lasted longer. He separated flowers from foliage, sorted them into colours and graded them by size.

As he placed the first glowing bloom in the chunky cut-glass vase, Ray smelt acrid shit cutting through heavy scent of freesia. Dawn's legs sticking out between the end of the worktop and the bin, a film of thin brown slurry coating her face. To her left four tiny crenellated marble islands protruding from the mire, to her right lay soggy wrapping paper, two sodden brochures and a soiled furl of bubble pack. The rooks had come.

Ray knelt and took her wrist. Nothing. He put his hand on her neck. Still no pulse. Her face cold and stiff, her eyes wide open and her hair matted with faeces. Ray lifted her limp body, hoisted it over his shoulder and carried her upstairs.

He took her into the bathroom, ran a bath, then cradled her in like baptism. Ray peeled away Dawn's stinking clothes, removed his own shoes, socks, trousers, shirt, underpants, and wriggled in beneath her. She lay in the water on top of Ray while he washed her body. He told her how beautiful she was and held her till the water cooled.

Ray laid Dawn out on the bed, towelled her dry, combed out her hair and eased her stiffening corpse into the brand-new velvet dress. He fetched fresh clothes for himself, buttoned his new silk shirt and phoned an ambulance.

Ray had to wait three hours after the service before the bereavement officer brought her out. He handed Ray a ten-inch grey-green cylindrical screwtop polytainer, which he explained was fully biodegradable, and went on to reassure Ray as a matter of procedure that the ash it contained stood no chance of being adulterated with any other remains since this was a state-of-the-art, completely modern facility in which the cremulator was dismantled and meticulously cleaned after each and every operation.

He informed Ray that the material contained therein was now his property to retain or to dispose of as he saw fit but felt it was his duty to caution him against any act, quite possibly heartfelt or inspired by grief, that might offend public decency or which he would later come to regret. Ray thanked him. The bereavement officer conveyed his deepest sympathies and left Ray to it.

Ray put Dawn in the glove compartment and drove out to the country. He parked by the pub, picked his way along the rocky shoreline and chose a spot where a narrow beck surged into the reservoir.

Ray twisted the top off the polytainer and caught a whiff of blood and bone. He poured her gritty dust onto the flow and watched the current sweep her away.

Dawn spread as the beck dissipated into the margins of the vast blank sheet of water. A shoal of roach churned the surface, wolfing her down.

A Note on the Author

Born in Leicestershire, Simon Crump studied philosophy at Sheffield University and has lived in Sheffield for the last twenty years. An internationally exhibited artist, he has lectured in fine art and photography at various universities and more recently worked as a curatorial assistant in a medical museum. His stories have appeared in numerous magazines and anthologies. He is the author of *My Elvis Blackout*.